E-GIRL

A TRANSGENDER ROMANCE TALE

NIKKI CRESCENT

HONEY HUT PUBLISHING

NEWSLETTER

JOIN NIKKI CRESCENT'S MAILING LIST!

Thank you for picking up one of my books! Chances are I'm in the process of working on another one! Hey—Did you know that you can read my whole catalogue free if you subscribe to **Kindle Unlimited**? It's true! If you aren't subscribed, I would highly recommend it.

I have started this little newsletter to let all of my beautiful readers know when I'm offering discounts, releasing new books, and giving away **EXCLUSIVE CONTENT FOR FREE**. The sign up takes about four seconds (seriously). I will never share your email address with anyone, you will never receive any spam, and you can unsubscribe at any time with the click of a single button.

CLICK HERE TO SIGN UP FOR NIKKI CRESCENT'S MAILING LIST NOW!

Can't open the link? Just copy and paste this link into your browser:

http://eepurl.com/O3CKz

COPYRIGHT

COPYRIGHT INFORMATION

FIND ME ON PATREON!

I really hope that you're enjoying my work! I've been fortunate enough to make this my full-time job for the past couple of years, though it hasn't been easy. There's a lot of financial uncertainty as a full-time self-published writer.

I would feel tremendously blessed if you would venture on over to my Patreon page and consider supporting me there. I think you will be excited by what I have to offer: **a community, free book chapters, pictures, contests, commissions, free stories, advanced releases, and much more**. It's the only way to get your hands on these exclusive titles:

THE PUNISHMENT
FORCED

TWINS
LORI'S LAST FUCK
THE GIRL TWIN (A Full-Length Novel)
TRANS CAM WHORE
GETTING READY FOR PROM
DUBIOUS CONSENT
PETRA'S FRISKY PHOTOSHOOT
JILLIAN'S 14 INCHES

And for as little as a dollar per month—is that even a quarter cup of Starbucks coffee?
Be the gorgeous, filthy doll you know that you are and come hang out with me:

https://www.patreon.com/nikkicrescent

DEDICATION

To the real Tuesday,

You can wear my lingerie anytime!

Love,

Nikki

E-GIRL

John devoted a huge chunk of his life to trying to be a professional gamer: a pursuit that was mocked by many, including his own parents. Now, in his thirties, with a wasted decade behind him, he's starting to realize that maybe the critics were right to mock him. He's jobless, has no degree, and he's single… but there is a girl.

John has played with Billie Rae online a few times. She's sweet, funny, and the two play well together… until they discover that they live in the same city. Then, Billie Rae gets uncomfortable and ghosts John. At least that's how it seems—and then a wealthy entrepreneur reaches out to John; he wants John on his new pro gaming team. It's a shocking dream come true for John—and it's an even bigger shock when he moves into the team house and meets his new teammates.

One is a beautiful, petite E-Girl. She's sweet, funny, talented... and it turns out, John already knows her; he's played with her many times before. His new teammate is Billie Rae. And John doesn't know it just yet, but he might just know Billie Rae even better than he realized.

CHAPTER 1

When I saw that little circle next to her gamertag turn green, a smile came quickly onto my face. I knew I had to act fast, to invite her into a game before she joined one on her own. "Hey," I wrote quickly. "Remember me?"

After I sent the message, I realized that I was possibly coming off as desperate, messaging her within seconds of her sitting down at her computer. I probably should have played it cool, and maybe waited for her to finish a game or two before inviting her to play with me... Now, I could just imagine her sitting there, rolling her eyes, thinking, 'Another creep...' She told me when we created a party together a few days earlier that guys were always being creepy with her, always hitting on her, always begging her to play with them.

And who could blame them? She was cute. She was your classic E-girl: cat-ear headphones, blush under her eyes, button-red nose, freckles (possibly fake, but cute nonetheless)… She had a stream, but she didn't link it to me. I badly wanted to ask her for her stream name, but I didn't want her to think that I was one of the creeps she told me about.

I had to play it cool with her if I wanted to play with her at all. Now, after sending that fast message, I had a feeling that I'd already ruined something that could have been a good gaming relationship…

And then she replied. "Hey! Of course I remember you. I'm just about to start streaming, but maybe we can play another game later."

I replied with a simple thumbs-up emoji, not wanting to come across as too desperate. Then, I went and joined a game of my own, with no party. We never did play a game that evening; our games just didn't line up. You know how it is: I finish one game just as she starts another. I took a short smoke break, hoping to return and see her in the lobby, but again, she'd already started another. She had hundreds of people on her friends-list; getting in with her was going to be tricky.

It didn't happen that night. I didn't think too much into it; it's not like I was in love with the girl. I didn't even know her. I played half a dozen games with her one night. But for some reason, I couldn't stop thinking about her. I just kept checking her in-game status. And my heart fluttered into the pit of my stomach when I saw her status turn from green to grey; she was offline.

Oh well… I just went on with my night.

There were other gamer girls out there—especially playing League of Legends. In fact, it was very in-vogue with girls. Pulling up the list of streamers playing the game showed thousands of them. I'd gone through pages of girls looking for her, but never was able to find her page. Maybe she streamed on a different website.

The next morning was my third day on the job, working retail at Game Stop. It was a minimum-wage job with no benefits aside from an employee discount, but for me, it was a dream job. I shouldn't say that the employee discount was the only perk; there was one little thing about the job that was a big deal to me…

"The Fatal Attack 3 shipment just came in," my boss said. "We can't sell copies until tomorrow, but we can load up the demo so it's ready for tomorrow."

That's right: I got to play Fatal Attack 3 before anybody else in that whole city. To me, that was a big deal. I got to experience that game before all of the guys who would be lining up in the morning to play it. To all of those guys, I was like a god. They would come in and I would be able to smile and tell them, "Yeah, it's good."

My boss even told me to stick around after my shift, to play it for an hour or two, so that I could give customers an honest review when they asked.

We were one of four game shops in that city. I was one of maybe a dozen people in a population of one million to play before launch. I got to hold that box in my hands and really see that artwork as it was meant to be seen.

Okay, so maybe that doesn't seem like such a big deal to you… or to most people. Maybe you would rather be earning a decent wage, or have medical benefits or insurance or a job that would cover future education to some degree. But for me, being able to experience a game like Fatal Attack 3 before anyone else… that was worth more than any insurance plan.

Okay, maybe I shouldn't say I got to play it before anyone else. Rick was the senior manager of the store: a young guy who started working there at sixteen. Now, at twenty-two, he was practically a pro. He knew everything about every video game. He truly had the dream job—maybe only making four or five bucks more than me per hour… but he got to set up at the conventions. He got to go to the annual Game Stop Christmas party in LA (all expenses paid). He even got a copy of Terrestrial Warriors a week before it arrived in stores, because the game makers wanted shops to start hyping the game early.

To me, Rick was like a god... and to think that he was a whole ten years younger than me, looking like a fresh-faced teenager. I suppose you could say that I was jealous.

He stayed after his shift with me to test out Fatal Attack 3's multiplayer mode.

He was good with his hands. It almost seemed like he'd played that game before... as if he'd been playing it for years. He creamed me, round after round. I was hardly able to get a hit in on him. He knew all the tricks. "How the hell are you doing that?" I asked.

"The mechanics are a lot like Justice Man," he said bluntly. "It almost seems like they recycled the engine... Probably because they had so many complaints about the mechanics of Fatal Attack 2. Seems like a really cheap workaround. When games cut corners like this... it never bodes well for the overall product." And I would have liked to call him a know-it-all... but his mastery of the game suggested that he knew what he was talking about.

He smoked me in ten straight bouts before putting the remote down. "Alright, I think I've seen enough. I should be running." He smiled at me. "I'm going to grab a Starbucks. Want one?"

"Thanks, Rick," I said. "One of these days, you're going to have to teach me how you play like that."

It wasn't just Fatal Attack 3. We'd played a few games together in my few days at the shop, and he creamed me consistently: brutal ass-whooping after brutal ass-whooping. It didn't seem to matter the genre: FPS, RTS... he even creamed me in the new farming simulator's new multiplayer mode.

He just smiled at me and then took off for the night.

I stayed there until 9:00 PM when the mall was closing, in that back room, playing Fatal Attack 3 on the demo machine. Then, I pulled it out into the shop, ready for opening in the morning, and I took off for home.

I lived with my parents; I'm sure that doesn't surprise you. I didn't make enough to rent a place on my own. I was saving up for college; my parents told me that if I wanted to go to college, I was on my own... but they also told me that I couldn't take out a loan; my dad didn't believe in student loans (or college in general). "You aren't burdening yourself for life with a useless degree." His way of stopping me from burdening myself was threatening to kick me out of the house if I dared to take out a student loan.

I know what you're thinking: a man in this thirties: uneducated, living with his parents, working at a video game store... maybe I wasn't the catch of a lifetime...

All of my friends from high school were married, had kids, had good careers. Hell, Samuel Carlson was retired already; he sold his tech company at thirty-two, made twenty-two million dollars, and decided that was enough work for him.

My best friend in high school, Derek Lee, no longer talked to me. He had four kids and lived in the suburbs. Now, he had a big dad-gut and had an Instagram where he posted about barbecue accessories.

And there I was, doing the same thing that I was doing when I was eighteen: playing League of Legends. I suppose I wasn't doing the same exact thing now... Now, I was playing much more casually: maybe four hours a night at most. Back in my twenties, I was logging fourteen hours per day, minimum. I had a dream of going pro. I was sure that I would make it onto a competitive team, play in tournaments, win my own millions.

You might be rolling your eyes right now, but those gamer guys really do make some serious bank at those tournaments. I took a trip out to San Diego to watch the Worlds, and the winning team left with eight million dollars in prize money—not a bad haul for a few guys to split up. Those guys won a few other tournaments that same year. The leader of their crew, Dizzy, posted a video walkthrough of his new home in Las Vegas: sixteen bedrooms and two swimming pools.

I wanted to be like them. I devoted my twenties to reaching that dream while my friends were courting women, studying in school, travelling the world.

In the end, I was left behind... I never made it to that level, though I'd gotten close once. I went to a tournament: they invited the top fifteen-hundred players, and I was player number-fourteen-hundred-and-eighty-eight. It was an elimination-style tournament, with the top hundred players earning a spot at the next tournament...

I finished #106. I was so close. I beat myself up about it for a long time... And then I was convinced that I could get back to that tournament to try again.

But the next year, I missed the cutoff… I was ranked #1,850. I never got that chance again… But I kept trying, year after year.

I was invited to tryout for Team Razor when I was twenty-nine. I practised for twenty hours per day. They needed two new players to complete their roster. Thirty guys were invited to tryout. I made it to the final day of tryouts; it was between me and four other guys… but I didn't make the cut. I made a stupid accident, trying to push the middle lane while the enemy team pushed bottom. My teammates yelled at me to help them stop the opposing push, but I was sure that I could divert them with my own push. I was sure that I could break them up before they reached our tower…

Nope. We lost the game and I was blamed. I didn't get a spot on that team.

My thirtieth birthday was a sad day. It wasn't where I imagined myself at thirty: jobless, broke, not on any team, now ranking around 9,000. There were so many great up-and-coming players, and I just wasn't one of them.

But I kept trying.

Now, I felt like a nobody. I felt like a failure. Everyone always says to chase your dreams, but chasing my dreams got me nowhere. Sometimes, it didn't seem like I had a whole lot to look forward to…

So when I saw her gamertag coming online that night, I did it again. "Hey, want to play a game?" I wrote quickly, before she even had a chance to join the queue. I probably looked desperate. I probably looked like one of the creeps that she told me about. Maybe I was one of those creeps… But I just felt like *something* had to come out of fourteen years of devoting myself to that damned video game. Maybe it wasn't some legendary career as a pro gamer. Maybe it wasn't millions of dollars from winning tournaments.

Maybe I could at least scrape away with a girlfriend…

CHAPTER 2

*O*kay, okay—I know what you're thinking: 'My God, this loser sure is a sad, desperate disgrace of a human'. At least that's how I was starting to feel about myself, especially when I saw Jeremy Erskine posting on Facebook, announcing that his wife was pregnant with their third baby. They'd just moved into a beautiful farm house in a very wealthy area. They'd clearly hired a professional photographer to take some maternity photos of them...

Meanwhile, my Facebook photo was from ten years earlier, of me holding a beer and standing next to a guy whose name I couldn't even remember. He was black-out drunk with a penis drawn on his forehead with a Sharpie, and I had the Sharpie in my free hand. I didn't even look the same in that photo as I did now. Back then, I had long hair and a hairless face. I had a youthful glow, full of potential. I was wearing newer clothes... now, my wardrobe was filled with those same old shirts and jeans, now tattered and worn, looking more like rags with each passing day.

That same photo was my gamer profile picture. I knew that I probably needed to update it, but I didn't have a better picture of myself. I never found myself at those gatherings where people were taking photos—and selfies just never worked out for me. They always came out awkward... embarrassing. Now, if I wanted to have any chance with this streamer chick, I needed to have a half-decent picture.

I was shocked when she replied. "Sure, let's play a game together. You don't mind if I stream it, do you?"

I felt tingly all over. I blushed. My fingers trembled. It was a familiar nervousness; I played with that same nervousness when I botched that tournament... and when I botched my pro team tryout. But now, I was nervous over a girl... a girl that I didn't even know. I knew her voice from playing with her one night, a few nights earlier. I vaguely knew what she looked like from her little profile picture. Otherwise, I knew nothing.

"I don't mind," I said.

"Your voice will be in the stream," she said. "Just so you know. I don't know how you feel about that."

"I don't care," I said.

She sent me a blushing emoji, and that was enough to make me blush. Why was she sending me that? Now, she was writing a message. I could feel beads of sweat forming on the back of my neck.

Why was I so nervous? Well, because she was out of my league. That little profile picture was more than enough to see that she was well, well out of my league. She was a decade younger than me. She had fans. She had men swooning over her.

"The stream tonight is a bit… racy. You don't mind being, uh, associated with that. Do you?"

"Racy?" I said. "What does that mean?"

"It's this thing I do on Fridays. I stream in lingerie. I know it sounds creepy, but it's not like porn or anything."

"Whatever," I said, trying to play it cool as my heart raced and my skin turned hot. "You do what you have to do."

Now, I really wanted to ask her what her stream was called, so I could look it up. I will admit, that while I was waiting for our first game to load, I minimized my game screen and searched through Twitch's stream listings, looking for a girl in lingerie playing League of Legends. I searched and searched, and then our game started so the search had to end.

My heart was racing, hearing her voice in our group chat, knowing what nobody else in that game knew: the user with the screen name 'BR-Cat' was actually a chick in skimpy underwear, streaming for the world to watch.

I was on-edge, knowing that there wouldn't be a game-two if I didn't perform to my best ability. It was a ranked game, meaning the outcome of that game actually affected our records. We were both ranked high, in the top 2% of all the players in that game (and it was, at that time, the most popular PC game on the planet). I was also trying hard not to breathe heavily into the microphone, or to let my voice crack as I played with that beautiful girl…

At least, I assumed she was beautiful; she was playing in lingerie with fans watching… Surely, she wasn't some slag. Or maybe she was… Maybe she put on the tight lingerie to compensate. Or maybe she had one of those fetish streams where she stuffed cake into her face while making her gut jiggle around…

No—that voice had a serenity to it. It had a soft-ness that made me sure that she was beautiful.

The game was off to a rough start, and it was my fault; I was playing a tricky role called jungle. Look —the game mechanics are irrelevant; long story short, it was my job to sneak around on the enemy side, snagging as many of their experience points and money as possible—but I went a bit further than was generally advisable. I took a big risk and got caught by two of their players. I was the first one to die, giving away precious experience points and money... and then, in an attempt to catch up quickly, I got caught a second time, being killed by the same player.

It was such a rough start that our teammate playing mid yelled, "What the actual fuck are you doing, you moron!?"

We were down 0-2, and it wasn't looking great after that. Now, they had a player who had the extra experience of two early kills. He was already two levels higher than everyone else in the game. He put those extra skill points into an ability that made him move faster, and he used that quick speed to catch one of our teammates out of position, killing him.

Now we were down 0-3, and I was blamed for

that third point… because it was technically my fault for letting that enemy get that 'overpowered'.

"I'm sorry," I said to BR-Cat, the lingerie-clad streamer.

"It's okay. We can bounce back," she said. She was the only optimistic one on the team… and she was the only one outplaying the opposing player in her lane. Five minutes into the game, she scored our first big point, taking down the enemy tower in her lane before sneaking away from a five-player ambush.

I must be tripping you up with all of these game details; I assure you that they're not important. All you really need to know is, we were losing, but BR-Cat, by female teammate, was giving us a fighting chance. She took that money from downing that tower to buy a weapon that made her stronger, and then she managed to catch one of the enemies out of position. Now, it wasn't looking so bad.

I knew that I had to play a perfect game from that point on; I couldn't be the reason for another lost point. I focussed hard on playing my part, intensely focussed on chipping away in that jungle area of the map. I was essentially nickel-and-diming my way back into the game—and it worked; I managed to catch one of their players attempting to sneak across the map to join in on an ambush. I slowed him and then I chipped away at him. He didn't put up a fight; he knew I would win in a one-on-one, but he tried to pull me towards his tower, which would have killed me... but I got him before he reached that tower: a fireball to the back. I vanished before his teammates came to help. I not only got that kill, but I spoiled their ambush.

Now, it was an even game, and I was part of the rally.

After breaking up the ambush, BR-Cat was able to take out another tower. But she didn't stop there; instead of retreating to heal up, she snuck into the enemy jungle and picked off some of their creeps, going unnoticed—because BR-Cat was smart; she knew that their 'jungler' was dead, still in the reincarnation queue. She was a savvy player, with great game sense; she had tabs on every player so that she wouldn't be caught off-guard. She knew their characters; she recognized what they were buildings towards. "Their support bought a staff," she said—and to most people, that wasn't relevant information, but she knew that it meant their support didn't have the cash to buy wards, which would normally be placed around the jungle to detect intruders like her. It was game-knowledge like that that made her a frightening force. The enemy assumed that she'd gone back to our base to heal up, but instead, she was grinding: gaining experience and money, and they had no clue. So when they finally encountered her again, a few minutes later, she was a few levels higher than all of them, with gear they absolutely were not anticipating. She struck them down and demolished them… and now, she was only becoming more powerful.

The enemy tried to stage five-man ambushes on her, but they all failed. And while they were making those attempts on her life, the rest of us were picking off creeps, taking out towers, inching up the map towards the enemy base.

We didn't make it to their base before the notification came on the screen: 'The enemy is voting to surrender'. It was only about five seconds before the vote was finished and the green letters came on our screens: VICTORY.

CHAPTER 3

*I*t wasn't until the dust had settled, and I heard her say, "Well played, John," that I remembered that I was playing with a lingerie-clad streamer. I guess the intensity of the game made that little anxiety flutter away; now, it was coming back with a vengeance. I blushed. Thankfully, she couldn't see my face… but she did hear my voice crack when I said, "It was all you, honestly."

She giggled: a sweet sound that lifted my heart up. A moment later, I was back on Twitch, trying to look for a stream that matched the criteria: lingerie-clad e-girl, playing League of Legends, currently in queue to start a new game. There were many e-girls, many playing League of Legends— and many of them were in lingerie. A few were in the queue as well—but none of them were in parties with myself.

So where the hell was she streaming? Or was the stream over now?

"Still doing your stream?" I asked.

"Yup," she giggled. "In fact, I should probably answer some viewer questions. You don't mind, do you?"

"No. Do your thing."

She definitely wasn't lying to me; I could hear those streaming sounds: the casino-esque sound effects blinging and chiming: ka-chinging as men dropped tips, blooping as they publicly send flirtations, cheering as new subscribers joined, dining as curious boys joined the stream.

I couldn't see the questions she was getting, but I heard her answers. At first, they seemed harmless. She was naming game characters. She said something about graduating college earlier that year. She talked about a childhood pet… and then she suddenly said, "If I had to pick, I would pick the pink vibrator." She giggled in a flirty way as my face turned dark red. Now, I was really trying to find this stream. I tried an alternate website that was just for streamers who got too racy for Twitch, but still couldn't find her. Where the hell was she!?

"You'd have to leave a really nice tip if you want me to do that," she said to one of her viewers. "Okay, okay. If I win the next game, I'll put it on. But only for one game!"

Put what on? What was she agreeing to? My heart was racing, but I tried to keep my cool. I remembered her telling me about the creeps... I didn't want to be one of them; I didn't want her to delete my name from her contact list. I wanted to play with her again, and not just because she was insanely good at the game.

We played three more games together. We won all of them. Each time, she was the MVP, though I did come close to getting a better score than her in that final game.

But the games were hardly relevant; it was the chatter between the games, while she was taking 'breaks' from streaming. "You don't mind waiting while I have a smoke, do you?" she would say—but I was thrilled that she wanted to stop gaming and streaming. She kept her Bluetooth headset on and we would chat while she stood out on her balcony. It almost felt like I was there with her, with my own wireless headset on, standing on my own balcony, taking drags from my own cigarette. I tried hard not to ask her too many personal questions. I was still worried about categorizing myself as a stalker or a creep.

"I like playing with you," she said to me with a smile in her voice. "You take crazy risks, and that just makes the game seem… less repetitive."

My heart skipped a beat as I smiled. I thought that she was going to delete me over my risk-taking.

"I've been playing this game since I was nine," she said. "And over the past year, I've really been thinking of leaving it behind for something new… maybe taking a break from it… But I've just put so much time into it. I would hate to just leave all of that hard work behind, with nothing to show for it."

My skin tingled all over. It was a familiar sentiment. "I know exactly how you feel," I told her, and then I told her about my decade of trying to go pro.

"You were at that tournament?" she said. "I was too."

"You were!?" I said. To be fair, there were fifteen hundred people there… but to think that I would have seen her in that huge conference centre… "I didn't realize you were trying to make this a serious career. I thought you were just a streamer… I mean —you're good at the game, so I guess I shouldn't be too surprised."

"I think I used to be better," she said. "With all the updates… sometimes I feel like I've been left behind."

We talked about the game for a long while. Then, suddenly, we were talking about old friends from high school. At times, it was like talking to myself, like when she said, "My best-friend from the ninth grade just got married, and she's pregnant now." BR-Cat was feeling left behind, just like me. Maybe we had more in common than we both realized.

It turned out, we had a lot in common, "I mean, people out here in Alberta tend to get married young —younger than the rest of the country—but it still feels like everyone is moving forward with their lives, and I'm just stagnating in the same place."

"Wait," I said, heart aflutter. "You're in Alberta? I'm in Alberta."

"Really?" she asked.

And then there was a long silence. My heart roared up against my ribcage. Maybe fate did have a hand in the past ten years of my life. Maybe it wasn't all a waste. Maybe it was all just leading up to this point, right now…

No—I couldn't get ideas like that in my head; I couldn't become some creepy stalker and ruin everything. I hardly knew this girl. I didn't even know what she looked like. I had to play it cool. She was silent now, probably terrified that I was going to be the worst stalker of her life. Her last stalkers were probably in other provinces, maybe in other countries...

I had to play it cool.

So I cleared my throat. "Up for another game?" I asked.

"I should probably do some other stream stuff," she said. "But, uh, it was nice playing with you, John."

"You too..." I paused, realizing I didn't know her name—just her gamer ID. "Um, do you mind if I ask your name?"

There was a short pause. She was probably considering her options... or maybe she was conjuring up a fake name to give me.

"It's Billie," she said softly. "Billie Rae. Anyway, I should go. Have a good night, John."

She left the party, and then I returned to my computer to see that message: BR-Cat left your group. I didn't jump back into another game. Instead, I searched for her stream. I tried to find her, so I could know what she looked like... but it was a waste of time. I spent an hour looking and finding nothing.

Maybe that was for the best. Maybe it was the universe telling me to stop obsessing over her... but it was hard to stop thinking about her. When I imagined her voice, I got goosebumps all over. I would find myself grinning, and blushing... and then I would remember her talking to her fans, talking about putting on lingerie. My mind was ripe with imagery, even though I had no idea what she looked like.

I shook my head and pushed those thoughts away.

I didn't want to become what people online called 'a simp'. A simp is a guy who swoons hopelessly over a woman, or over multiple women. He showers her with compliments and tries to force himself into her online presence, thinking that it might get him somewhere. A simp is a sad, desperate person... and sadly, I'd been there before, around the time I turned thirty, when my life was particularly hopeless.

I'll tell you a little bit about it, but I hate to. It was an embarrassing time in my life, but it ended with me getting the reality slap that I probably needed to get many years earlier.

There was a girl named Wendy; I don't think it was her real name. She posted selfies on some Reddit page, every day. "What do you think of my makeup?" she would ask in the caption. "Do I look cute today?" "Would you ask me out?" "Still waiting for the boys to notice me." She was a stunning redhead with amazing freckles. "I'm feeling lousy. Can someone please tell me I look cute?"

I would see that she wasn't getting any comments, and I was stunned, thinking men were crazy to not notice her... so I gave her the attention. "Beautiful, as always," I would write. I thought I was just being sweet. She would message me back. "Thanks so much. You're such a sweetheart." And she made me feel like I was actually cheering her up, actually lifting her up her spirits.

She started to chat with me away from the

comments sections. I told her my name and she would message me in the morning, "Good morning, John!" Soon, she wasn't posting selfies on that Reddit page. Instead, she would send them to me for the validation she was looking for.

"You seriously look so cute," I would say.

She would send back blushing emojis and thank me. I looked forward to our quick morning chats.

And then she started telling me about the issues in her life. I felt like she was opening up to me. She linked me to her Instagram page, where she was trying to become a model. She told me how Instagram's algorithm worked, and I told her that I would help her by liking and sharing and favouriting and commenting everything—as much as I could. I noticed there were many other guys posting comments like mine. I asked her if she had a boyfriend, and she told me that she was single, that a few guys had broken her heart in the past.

"I would never do that," I told her.

I found out she lived in Vancouver, because I recognized a few buildings in a few of her pictures. So I decided to make the trip out, to meet with her. We had a whole week planned together, but when I pulled up to her building, she messaged me and told me that she was ill, and the virus was contagious. "I'm so sorry, John. We'll have to reschedule."

But I was already there.

Two months later, I made the trip out again, ready to take her to the aquarium, to the zoo, to the boardwalk, to the theatre. But this time, she got called in to work the day I was supposed to meet her... and then she had to fly to Winnipeg for a funeral. I tried to catch her at the airport, but I couldn't find her before her plane left.

Then she told me that she was struggling financially, so I sent her some cash...

Okay, so I'm guessing you know where this is going. There's a reason I don't tell people this story; because as soon as I start telling it, people plant their faces into their palms and they shake their heads, as if I'm some big, dumb doofus idiot. And yeah, I guess I was. Desperation will do that to a guy.

I sent her a few thousand dollars, thinking I would help her out of a jam...

A month later, I sent her more. Then I sent her a bit more...

And then, one night while I was feeling particularly lonely... and horny, I went to a new Reddit page and I saw her picture, being posted with a new account, posting similar captions, fishing for another man to give her the treatment I'd been giving her.

Was she a catfish or just a scammer? I never did find out… I stopped communication with her and I just accepted the losses. It's not the proudest moment of my life… And I guess it's even more embarrassing to admit that it happened again a few months later: another three-thousand dollars washed away before I realized I was being scammed again… this time by someone that I actually met, in person, in Edmonton. We went for dinner together, and she even gave me a kiss… I guess her scam was just much more intricate and involved.

Anyway… long story short: I knew what it was like to be desperate, and I knew that it never led to good things. Now, there was even a part of me wondering if Billie Rae was a scammer. I'd heard stories about them being on League of Legends. Guys getting their girlfriends to wear their headsets while they play. They get men to buy them loot in the game… and sometimes outside of the game. Maybe Billie Rae was just building me up, putting images in my head of some vixen in lingerie. Maybe she knew that I was in Alberta before she let that little nugget of information slip. Was it in my profile bio somewhere? Was she able to check my IP address?

That's what being scammed three times had done to my confidence…

Okay, yes—it happened a third time. Let's not talk about that anymore.

I no longer believed a girl could actually like me… not a girl like Billie Rae, anyway…

I shook my head, trying to expel those negative thoughts. I didn't even know what the girl looked like! Maybe she was a troll. Maybe she just had a pretty voice. Maybe she streamed her body and kept her face out of it because she had yellow, crooked teeth and a giant hook nose, beady eyes, and a the wrinkled forehead of a seventy-year-old smoker… Then, maybe she would be in my league…

No—there was that negativity again. I'd spent the past few years trying to pull myself out from that mental rut. I was better than that. I was worth more than that…

I was just about to go to bed when my gaming inbox dinged. "If you're around tomorrow night, let's play again," she wrote to me. She was already offline by the time I finished reading.

The smile on my face only lasted a few seconds. It was hard not to think about those scammers.

CHAPTER 4

*R*ick was working the floor when the copies of Dance Party 2023 came into the store. It was one of the most anticipated games of the year… not my thing; I'd never been into those platform games, and I definitely wasn't a dancer… but it was still cool holding that game in my hands four days before we would put the game would be on the shelves.

Rick was staring at the box art with a smile on his face. "Better cover than last year," he said.

"You into those games, Rick?" I asked with a teasing grin.

He shrugged his shoulders. "Sure. Why not? They're fun."

I was surprised. I wasn't even blushing. I couldn't imagine him dancing. He just seemed like a big nerd, like me... though he was quite a bit more handsome than me. Girls were often coming in and flirting with him, though he never seemed to notice as he would push back his long dark hair from his face. He had those boyish good looks that every guy wishes they have in high-school. It was hard not to roll my eyes sometimes when the girls would come in and dart right past me to ask him about the new releases.

He looked into my eyes with a big grin. "Are you going to stay late to test this one?" he asked, holding that game up.

I laughed. "Probably not this one," I said.

"Too manly to dance, John?" he asked with a chuckle as he turned back to unpacking the box.

"It's just not my thing," I said.

"What's your game of choice?" he asked.

"Well," I said. I usually didn't tell people about my commitment to League of Legends. I didn't like admitting that I wasted a decade of my life. I didn't like getting into it; it was a sore topic... but sometimes it was hard to talk about other stuff... because I didn't have much else to talk about at that point in my life. Most of my adult life had been spent committed to that one goal... and most people thought that goal was stupid, even back when I had the potential to go far. Now, it was especially stupid: a decade spent trying to go pro... and then failing.

"Too shy to tell me?" he said.

"Well, I'm a big fan of, uh, League of Legends."

Then, he perked up. "No way," he said. "Me too."

Lots of people were into it, so that wasn't much

of a surprise. I just smiled and nodded and said, "How long have you been playing?"

"Oh, a few years, I guess," he said. "Are you pretty good?"

"I like to think that I'm okay," I said. I decided not to tell him that I'd briefly been in the top 1,500 globally. I didn't want to brag... and I didn't want to admit that I'd had a major falling-from-grace. "You?"

"I'm okay, I guess," he said. "I'm not, like, pro or anything. Maybe we should play sometime."

"Sure," I said. I had a secondary account for playing casually—with no information linking me to my primary account... I didn't need people seeing that badge of shame, showing all of my logged hours, and all of those achievements that really meant nothing... all of those skins that I earned with hours, thinking that was better than using real money... but was it really? Is time not more valuable than cash? Those skins just represented my twenties, which I no longer had.

I tried to change the subject, asking Rick if he planned on staying at that shop or if he had biggest aspirations in his life. I tried to word it in a nicer way than that, of course; I did my best not to insinuate that his job was lousy and he needed to aspire to better things. I made sure to say, "You have my dream job, by the way."

He smiled and shrugged his shoulders. "I have goals, like everyone else," he said. But he was vague about those goals, giving me no more information, and I assumed that meant, 'Let's leave that topic alone'. Maybe his life wasn't quite as perfect as I assumed it was.

"Well, I plan on staying here," I said. "My family doesn't get it, but this is a dream for me."

He smiled, but there was a sadness behind that smile. "This job won't always exist, you know."

"What do you mean?"

"Well, just look at this," he said, holding up that dance game. "Do you know what's in this box?"

"No. What?" I said.

"Nothing," he said. "It's an empty box. There's a code inside of it. You can redeem that code online— but really, the box is pointless. Even buying this is pointless—and even kind of stupid, because it's just a matter of time before someone figures out the algorithm that they used to generate these codes, so that they can steal codes for themselves. It makes more sense to just buy yourself an instantly redeemable copy; that way you don't risk being ripped off. The only reason people buy these physical copies is so they can wrap them and give them as gifts…"

And it was a good point. People really didn't need to go into stores like that one for games, though lots of people still did… mostly older people who had grown up buying games in person. Now, that store also sold t-shirts and other game swag. It was more like a novelty store than a game store, but it was still primarily a game store… at least to me.

"Your nuts if you think this will still be a job in five years," Rick said. "So start coming up with a backup plan."

I didn't have any backup plan. My backup plan was to go through the mall dropping off resumes, praying one place would call me back… and then not ask in the interview why I had a ten-year gap in my work history.

Well, I suppose I did have a bit of a backup plan…

I hate to even admit this to you, after everything that I've told you…

But in the back of my mind, I still thought that there was hope of getting back into the top rankings on League of Legends. Every now and then, I would have an incredible win streak, and I would get to thinking, 'Maybe I could get back to that place…

Maybe I still have a shot at being on one of those pro teams one day…'

"So, if you were forced to do something else tomorrow, what would you do?" Rick asked.

I shrugged my shoulders. "I don't really know," I lied. I wasn't going to tell him about my League aspirations.

"Oh, come on, John. Tell me," he said. " I can see that glimmer in your eye. There's something."

I sighed, but I didn't tell him. I couldn't. I respected him too much. He was like the man I wished I could have been. He was cool. He was successful. He was good at video games. Girls liked him. I didn't want him to think that I was a loser.

"Okay, fine," he said. "You don't tell me, I won't tell you." He winked at me and then he began to unwrap one of the copies of the dance game to load into the demo machine. "I can't wait to give this a go later."

I thought that he was kidding about wanting to play the dance game. I thought he was just trying to get a giggle out of me, but then, that evening, I went into the back room and saw him testing it out. He turned and smiled at me. "It's fun," he said, without even blushing. "You should try it, John."

"It's not really my thing," I said.

"They've really improved it this year," he insisted. "It's a lot of fun. I bet you'd like it."

"I'm not a dancer," I said.

"Oh, come on, John! Quit being so shy and just try the damned game. In fact—that's an order, as your manager. Pick a song and dance. You need to know the game in case people ask questions about it."

I could feel myself turning red all over. I didn't have a choice: I had to test out the silly game, even if it meant humiliating myself in front of my boss... But I wanted him to think that I was cool, that I didn't get humiliated by having to dance. It was, after all, part of my job description: having to test out games.

I let Rick pick the song, pretending like I didn't care what he picked. He was going to be dancing next to me, after all. Well, to tease me, he picked Toxic by Britney Spears—and it was a sexy dance... very embarrassing, imitating the generated woman on the screen. There was one part where she bent over and shook her ass. I just stood there and laughed, accepting that I would lose points for not doing it... and then I looked over and saw Rick doing it... and nailing it with surprising accuracy. I will admit that I blushed, and he just smiled—and then he laughed at me, as if I was the one who should have been embarrassed.

I was red all over by the end of the song. Rick, as usual, creamed my score: quadrupling me. "Why are you so shy, John?" he asked. "It's just a game. Cut loose and live a little!"

"I guess dancing has just never been my thing."

"You weren't so bad there for a moment," he laughed. "Besides, one day a girl is going to want you to take her dancing. Knowing how to dance might get you laid." He winked and laughed.

It was a good point, but I don't think Toxic was the best starting point.

"Speaking of girls," he said. "You seeing anyone?"

I wanted Rick to think that I was cool, so I decided to exaggerate a little bit. "I have a date tonight," I said with a grin.

His eyes widened. "Really?"

"Really."

"What are you guys doing?"

"We're, uh, gaming. It's… a LAN party."

He had a crooked look on his face. "What's a LAN party?"

I guess that was an old term. Was there even such a thing as LAN anymore? I was dating myself. "We're going to, uh, get together and play a game."

"Oh, she's a gamer girl," he smiled. "Good for you. Is she cute?"

I couldn't admit I had no idea what she looked like. "She streams," I said. "She's pretty popular too."

He nodded his head. "So that means she must be cute?"

"Beauty is subjective," I said, trying to skirt around the question without having to lie.

"Well, I hope that goes well for you. You should take the demo." He held the demo box out to me. "Take it home and impress her with your dance moves." He winked at me. "And you can impress her by letting her play a game that's not even out yet."

"Is... Is that allowed?" I asked.

"As long as you bring it back," he said. "Like—seriously, bring it back. I'm not supposed to let you take the game home, unless it's necessary. In this case, I could lie and say that it's necessary, that you needed a bit of education on the topic. I don't mind pulling a few strings. You're a cool guy, John. And I trust you."

I felt myself turning dark red all over. Did Rick, the coolest guy in the mall, just call me... *cool*? I tried hard not to smile. "Thanks, but I don't think I'm hurting to do anymore dancing today. I don't think that's so much her thing either." I cleared my throat.

"What about you? Seeing any girls?" I'm sure he was seeing plenty of girls.

But Rick was modest. He just smiled and shrugged his shoulders. I knew what that meant; it meant that he was seeing lots of women, getting lots of action...

Oh well. Maybe one day I would be more like him.

It seemed so silly, but I really wanted to impress him. I was so tempted to tell him about how great I once was at League of Legends. I wanted to tell him about how I was invited to a serious tournament. Maybe then he would think that I was cooler than some guy nearing his mid-thirties, with no real achievements to show for nearly two decades of adult life...

I decided to keep my mouth shut. 'Almost' being great wasn't an achievement worth bragging about. I needed to do better than that.

And now, I could think of something worth bragging about: Billie Rae. No, I couldn't brag about her yet, because she wasn't mine... yet.

CHAPTER 5

I was online early, not joining into any games as I waited for her little circle to turn green. I was sitting upright, occasionally blurting out little vocal warmups like, "Unique New York. Unique New York..." I really felt like I was getting ready for a date... and it was the closest thing to a real date that I'd been on in almost five years—unless you count being on dates with scammers.

It was 9:00 PM when she finally came online. My heart skipped a beat. I'd been waiting for over two hours, just surfing the web as I tried to keep my nerves cool. I typed out a message but waited a few minutes before sending it. I didn't want to appear desperate. "Hey there," I finally wrote. "Fancy a game?" After I sent it, I felt like a complete idiot. 'Fancy a game?' What was I thinking? I may as well have written 'm'lady' after it! Oh God, she probably thought that I was sitting there in a fedora, scratching at the beard on my neck, sipping Mountain Dew and chowing on a pack of Doritos.

I was shocked when I got a reply from her.

"Sounds like fun. You don't mind if I'm streaming, do you?"

"Hey—you do you," I said. I don't know why I was putting so much effort into sitting upright. I'd even cleaned up my desk... and my room. I was wearing my nicest shirt, and I was actually wearing pants: a nice pair of jeans that made my figure look good... though I'd always found them to be a bit uncomfortable, so I almost never wore them.

It's not like she could see me. But I still felt like I needed to treat it like a date. Besides, the excuse to clean up my room wasn't necessarily a bad thing...

"How was your day?" I asked.

"Oh, it was okay," she said. "Same old... busy day at work. How was your day?"

She was preparing her stream: getting her room ready. She told me that she picked up some new shelves at a hardware store, but wasn't quite sure how to put them up. The goal was to put some video game swag on the shelves, to make her background a bit more appealing. "I want to do some under lighting... maybe with a soft pink," she said. "But I have no idea how to do any of that."

"If you want help," I said. "I used to do some construction stuff with my dad." My heart began to race. 'Play it cool,' I thought to myself. 'Just play it cool. Don't let her think that you're one of those creeps.'

She giggled. "I might take you up on that," she said. Now my heart was really racing. Was she serious, or was it just polite conversation?

I decided not to push it any further. "What do you think of the new heroes they released?" I asked, and now we were onto talking about the game. We chatted for thirty minutes before she booted up her stream. She warned me that my voice would be in the stream. "So be careful what you say," she said, and I swear I could hear her winking, as if she was insinuating that I might end up talking dirty with her.

It wasn't lingerie day on the stream now. It was, presumably, a normal day. By the sounds of it, she still had many viewers tuning in. I heard the dings and bloops and chimes of her feed. She replied to the odd comment. After our first game, she explained to me that she was required to answer questions when people asked the question along with a tip. "Sorry if it seems like I'm talking over you when that happens," she said to me.

We were both having a smoke on our respective balconies when she asked me, "Do you have a girlfriend, John?"

"A girlfriend?" I asked, tensing up all over. "N—No. Not right now. Why?"

"I'm just wondering," she said. "You seem like a cool guy. I'm just surprised to hear that you don't have a girl in your life."

"I guess it just hasn't happened for me yet." I cleared my throat. "And you... do you have a boyfriend?"

There was a long silence. Now, I wanted to take the question back. My hands were trembling. I felt like a thirteen-year-old in school all over again.

"Nope," she replied. "I guess I've just been too busy with work and streaming."

"Where do you work?" I asked.

"Aren't you just full of questions today?" she said.

And again, I tensed up. I knew that I had to be careful not to push it, not to clump myself in with all of the men before me who tried and failed. "Sorry," I said.

"We should probably get back on the stream."

We played two consecutive games, winning both. With Billie Rae, I was lossless. I'd now played ten games with her and I hadn't lost a single one. At first, I thought that she was just pulling me, and then, during our next break, she told me that she'd never won so many games in a row before at such a high rank. "It's so good to have such a strong jungler," she said to me, making me blush. "We work really well together."

It was only a few minutes later that she was telling me about her childhood. She told me about her daddy taking her to the zoo. She told me about vacationing on Vancouver Island every summer, until she was sixteen. She cried when she told me about her mother passing away tragically on her eighteenth birthday. She was opening up to me... and I couldn't help but think that she was really starting to like me. She trusted me to be so open with me.

And I started opening up with her. We could have chatted all night long, but her stream was still waiting, so we had to go back to the game.

We won another pair of games decisively. Then, right before we took another break, I heard her gasp. "Whoa," she said.

"What is it?"

"My rank," she said. "It's gone way up. I don't think it's ever been this high."

So I checked my rank too. We were both around 1,600. My skin tingled. I'd been that high before... but it had been a long, long time. Now, I had a lump in my throat. Old ideas began to flutter into my head. Old dreams resurfaced as new possibilities.

Maybe there was still a chance of going pro. Maybe some team would notice me if I could crack that 1,500 barrier. I just needed to win another five or six straight games to get there... I could do it with Billie Rae.

We went out for one last smoke break. Then, after chatting about her childhood retriever for a few minutes, she said, "I think I should probably head off to sleep. I still need to sign off with the stream and get all of the links up on my social media pages for the replays."

"Don't you just want to stay up for a bit longer? We could play a few more games... without the stream." But now, I wasn't asking because I wanted to keep on chatting with her. Now, I was asking because I wanted her to help me make my rank soar. "I hope you don't mind me saying, but I think we make a really good team. I, uh, really like you, Billie. You're a cool girl. You're a lot of fun to hang out with. I wish we could do it in person."

There was a long, long silence. It was horrible... excruciating. Did I just ruin everything? Did she now think that I was hitting on her?

Was I hitting on her?

"I really had a long day," she said to me. "Sorry. Maybe we can play again another night. Good night, John."

And just like that, she was off. I tried to find her stream one last time, but it was hopeless: I couldn't find it anywhere, as if she was streaming on some alternate internet that I didn't know about.

I went to play a game without her, and suffered my first loss in three days. It was a close game, and the loss wasn't my fault... but it was still a loss. Now, my rank was back down to 1,900. It was almost 1:00 AM now. I tried to play one more round: another loss, dropping me to 2,050.

I could feel the air being sucked out of me as I deflated. The universe decided to tease me just a little bit... and now I was just back to where I was before. It was just rubbing my decade of failure into my face, mocking me for pursuing a career as a professional gamer. I went to bed defeated, feeling idiotic—and that feeling only got worse when I realized I probably ruined things with Billie Rae too. Near the end of the night, I was practically ignoring her; when she told me about her childhood dog, I was hardly listening, just staring at my new shiny rank and fantasizing about being great again. I'm sure she noticed. I'm sure that's why she cut me off so suddenly. And she didn't even give me a date to look forward to: no 'let's play again tomorrow.'... Just, 'maybe we can play again another night.'. It was a vague little rejection.

I ruined a good thing over some stupid fantasy that just wouldn't leave me alone.

Rick smiled at me when he saw me the next morning. "You look tired," he said with a grin. "Your date keep you up all night?"

I didn't want to admit that my 'date' was never a date at all, and she ditched me when I became obsessed with my League of Legends ranking. So I just smiled, trying to insinuate that I had a hot night without having to lie with my words.

"I'm proud of you," he said. "Did you end up dancing with her?"

"I didn't get around to it," I said.

"I'm telling you, John," he continued. "Dancing is fun. It's okay to look silly from time to time. Girls like it when you make yourself vulnerable."

"I'll keep that in mind," I said.

I was so wrapped up with my own stupid issues that it wasn't until around 10:00 AM that I noticed he had a beaming look on his blushing face. "How was your night?" I asked him.

"It was good," he said. And now, it looked like he

was hiding a big smile, containing a big announcement. Maybe he'd been waiting all morning for me to ask him what was new.

"What is it?" I asked.

"Well," he said. "I got an email this morning. It's, uh, for a job. And I'm thinking of taking it. Just thinking."

"A job?" I said.

"I probably shouldn't say anymore than that. My parents taught me not to brag about an achievement until it's actually an achievement."

"What does that mean?" I asked, scratching at the side of my head.

"You know," he said. "Like, don't go bragging to people that you've started some weight loss program until you've already lost the weight—kind of like that."

"Oh," I said. "So you aren't going to tell me about the job?"

"Maybe soon," he said. "Like I said: I don't know if I'm going to take it."

"Would you leave here if you did?" I asked.

"I would have to," he said. "But let's not talk about that right now. Like I said; it was just an offer."

I was happy for him... but also jealous, even though I had no idea what it was all about. I'd only known Rick for a little over a week, but I knew him well enough to know that if he was excited about something, it was probably something really cool. He already had an awesome life, and this was apparently something that would potentially make his life even more awesome.

Around noon, it occurred to me that his position would open up if he left. No, I wasn't next in line to be the manager, but it would mean moving up in seniority—something that I thought wouldn't happen for years. Carol would probably take his position, and then Andy would take Carol's spot—and then maybe I could have Andy's spot. It would mean a dollar raise—an extra eight bucks each day—forty bucks a week. That was enough for a few new skins on League of Legends… or maybe I could save it up so I could rent an apartment of my own one day, and stop being a bum in my parents' house.

But like Rick said: it wasn't something worth thinking about yet. It was just an offer, and he wasn't even sure if he was considering it. That was his business to think about, not mine.

While he was looking at a wonderful life improvement, I had problems to think about: a life that was creeping by while I stagnated: no girlfriend, no achievements, and a job at the mall that was usually reserved for teenagers... At least it was my dream job...

At least, I thought that it was my dream job. Now that I'd been there for a week, I was starting to wonder if this really was such a great job. That morning, we were tasked with clearing all of the vintage games off of the vintage game shelf. We needed to make room for a new shipment of novelty bobble-heads.

And now, there were rumours that we would soon be clearing out the Playstation wall so that we could expand our t-shirt selection. The XBOX wall would become the mixed-console wall. I was hardly working in a video game store anymore; now, it was more like some novelty gimmick shop that had a shrinking video game section. It wasn't the video game paradise that I remembered when I was a child, and I would go into that shop and stare in wonder at the walls of game artwork, at the flashing game demos, at the gods who were the lucky chosen ones to work in that heavenly paradise…

I thought that I would be one of those gods. I thought kids would come in and look up to me the way I looked up to Game Stop workers when I was a kid. But instead, they would roll their eyes if I tried to approach them. If I walked up to them and said, "Hey kids, have you tried this new game?" They would giggle at me as if I was a complete loser. Our boss told us to push those bobble-heads, but the kids weren't interested; the kids just wanted to browse through the T-shirts. "Does anyone even listen to these bands?" they would ask, and then they would leave the store laughing.

Our clientele was older: about my age. We mostly sold those bobble-heads to people who collected bobble-heads. I'm not one to pass judgement, but the average buyer was larger, usually either balding or with hair that hadn't been cut in over half a decade. Many wore fedoras. They would buy every single bobble head, even if it was from some game or show they didn't play or watch.

At the end of that day, our boss let us know that the shoe shop next door had inquired about expanding their stock room. They wanted to lease out our stock room, and my boss was now trying to figure out if we could shrink our shop to make room for a small stock area. "It would help to cut on the recent losses," he said. And I was suddenly realizing that Rick was right: this wasn't going to be a career. This job wouldn't be around in five years time. I would probably never make manager—and if I did, it would be a temporary gig at best.

I had no backup plan.

And at the very end of that day, I looked over at Rick and saw that he still had that gleam in his eye and that beaming look on his face. He was still thinking about that job offer; and how could he possibly turn it down now?

CHAPTER 6

BR-Cat was online that night, but I didn't message her. I didn't want to seem desperate, so I played alone. I won a few, lost a few. My rank stagnated. Then, I looked at her name again on that list and thought about messaging her. A: I wanted to hang out with her and find out if I ruined my chances with her; and B: I wanted her to help me boost my rank. We won together, and now, winning was more important than ever. Now, I had that idea back in my head: going pro was quite possibly my only ticket off of this sinking ship that I was stuck on.

Rick was right: Game Stop wouldn't be open in five years time, and I needed a backup. With no education and hardly any decent work experience, I was screwed. But if I could just go pro… if I could sneak onto a team.

See—maybe you know this or maybe you don't, but pro teams live together. They live in team houses that are paid for by the team sponsors. Everyone has their bedroom, and the living room is like a big gaming cafe, with rows of computers where the players train together, preparing for tournaments. It was my dream to live in one of those houses.

I found myself outside, on the balcony, staring out at the city skyline. I looked out at the sea of homes. There were so, so many of them: thousands, as far as the eye could see… and I didn't have one of my own. All of my old friends were in those homes, with their families, returning home from their careers…

I knew that my time was running out. I had one last shot at making something out of this professional gaming fantasy: one more month, and then I needed to move on. That was it. I wasn't going to let this fantasy hold me back any longer. It had taken enough of my life away. I would take it seriously for one more month, and then I would delete the game, sell my computer, flip through the community college catalogue with my eyes closed and pick a trade at random.

This was it.

Rick announced two days later that he would be leaving. I didn't get to see him again; our schedules didn't line up. He had already gone onto his new job and spent his final two weeks working part time on weekends, while I worked weekdays. Without Rick, work wasn't as much fun. My new manager, Chloe, was a growling feminist who scorned every man who came in to buy an anime poster featuring girls with big breasts.

She would start every shift by taking down the new releases from the shelf, putting up the latest woke titles in their place to give them more exposure, and then she would spend the end of each shift putting the new releases back up where they belonged, because those companies were technically paying for that front-of-store exposure. She went on and on and on about TV shows I'd never heard of. She hate nothing but garlic-sauce shawarmas for lunch, giving her an odour that nobody could stand... Okay, enough about Chloe. The point is: work was no longer enjoyable at all. But the dread of spending the day with Chloe provided me with the motivation I needed in the evenings to boost my rank. I managed to inch my rank back into the top 2000.

I WAS NO LONGER PLAYING with Billie Rae, though I always wanted to message her. Now, she was out of my league, ranked 1350 and climbing a little bit every day. I was too afraid of asking her to play, worried that I would drag her rank down. But the thought of catching up to her so that she would want to play with me again... that was even more motivation to work hard.

I spent that weekend playing like I used to: fourteen hours on Saturday, and then eighteen hours on Sunday. I inched my way up, up, up. I reached 1600… and then I hit 1550. My hands were trembling from playing for so long. My eyes were sore from staring at the screen.

But it wasn't for nothing.

My life changed that Monday morning. I woke up to a message from an unknown user. "Are you based out of Alberta?"

"Yeah, why," I replied.

I didn't get a response back until after work that evening. "I'm the owner of Centennial Greens," he said. "We're starting a professional gaming team. Two months ago, we purchased a property in Red Deer. It's an eight-bedroom home and the renovations are almost complete. We're looking to sign three new members to our competitive team."

It was the moment I'd been working towards for over a decade. No, it wasn't an established team with a trophy room and an alumni of legendary players… but it was still a team.

The message continued. "We've already been accepted to play in the National Qualifier. The Qualifier is in two weeks and training would start ASAP, if you're interested."

"Sign me up," I said. Was it the perfect offer? No —far from it... but it was a step in the right direction. It was further than I'd ever been. Nobody had ever offered me a spot on a team. This was my chance to prove something.

I called my boss at Game Stop and told them that I wasn't coming back into work. They told me that I couldn't leave without giving two weeks, unless I wanted to lose them as a name on my resume references. It was a risk that I had to take.

I packed up my bags. I told my parents that I was moving to Red Deer, two hours away. They were shocked. My dad gave me the familiar spiel about gaming not being a real career. But it was just more motivation; I would prove him wrong... finally.

The top eight teams at the National Qualifier would go on to play Nationals, and then the winner of Nationals would play the World Circuit. Every tournament in Worlds had million-dollar prizes. Even if we could just win one of those tournaments...

I got into my car that night and left for my new life. I drove in the night, in the rain, moving carefully in the slow lane so I wouldn't hydroplane off of the road and die before I could taste my fantasy.

I arrived at the mansion in Red Deer at 2:00 AM. The key box was on the door. I'd been given the code, and a room number. The code worked. The key was there. I stepped in and was struck by that new home smell—as well as the smell of computer parts and keyboard cleaning aerosol.

The place was dark, but I could see the computer room: the black silhouettes of desktop computers in that dark space. I took off my shoes and left my bags by the door, sauntering over. My heart was racing. I looked at those expensive monitors. The walls were covered in Centennial Green logos. It was a cannabis company. Monster Energy drinks had also agreed to be a sponsor. There were glowing Monster mini-fridges in the room, changing colour every few seconds. I couldn't wait to start playing.

I couldn't wait to meet my new teammates.

CHAPTER 7

My bedroom was upstairs, in the back corner of the house. It was a small room, like a bedroom you might find in a cheap Tokyo hotel. I didn't mind; I didn't need much personal space. The tiny bed was enough for me.

They provided white sheets and a single pillow; it was a bit stiff, but fine for me. I didn't get a great sleep that night, but not because the bed was lousy; I was just excited, restless, counting down the seconds until my career as a professional gamer would finally start.

Then, I woke up to the sound of laughing down-stairs. I rubbed my eyes, remembered the excitement of the previous day, and then I jumped to my feet. I scrambled into clean clothes and then I rushed down the stairs to meet my team.

There, standing in the room were four guys and two girls. They all stopped and turned to look at me. There was a moment of silence before I broke it by saying, "Are you guys my new teammates?" I felt myself blushing. They were all in pyjamas, sipping coffees. They seemed like cool people: all at least five years younger than me, fit, put-together. There was one guy with a long beard and a balding head, but he still had a strangely charming look about him. "Bruce," the bearded man said, extending his hand. "Team captain. My gamertag is Tank."

I knew Tank! He was ranked 600, but had flirted with the top 250 before. I suddenly felt like a fanboy, trying to hide my grin. I knew that I was blushing. "Hi," I said. "J-Rock. Uh, I mean John. J-Rock is my gamertag."

"Cool! We've played before," he said. It was true, but I was shocked that he remembered; it was almost five years earlier…

"Hi, J-Rock," said another man. He was short, but handsome, with long black hair that looked like male model hair. I suppose, by pro gaming standards, he was a pretty boy—though to normal folk he was probably just another nerd. "Roger. Race-Star on League."

"Race-Star!" I gasped.

He smiled with a modest, rosy look on his face. "You know me?"

"Of course I know you!" I said.

Then, I turned my gaze to the others. Franklin was the tall, skinny fellow with the glasses. He was shy, saying nothing but his name and his gamertag: Griswold Gamer. I'd never heard of him, but I didn't want to be rude by asking his rank.

Then there was Erin, a chunky girl with black hair and bad acne, but she still had a pretty face, with long lashes and piercing green eyes. "Kitten Krusader," she said. I'd heard of her, but she wasn't ranked high—not even in the top 3000. I was surprised to see her there.

Next stepped up Gregory, also known as Gobbler. He had a crooked grin on his face. His body was covered in tattoos, including a neck tattoo that said, 'Fuck Bitches'. He couldn't have been taller than five-two. "Nice to meet ya," he grinned.

"Likewise," I said. I'd heard of him too, but I had no idea where he ranked.

There was only one more person in that room: a blonde with pink highlights. She was wearing one of those fluffy, baggy hoodies with the cat ears on the hood—one of those outfits that all the E-girls wear. She was wearing a tiny pair of booty shorts, showing off her big League of Legends thigh-piece.

She had big eyes... scared eyes. She was frozen. Her skin was pale... or maybe she was just very, very fair...

"Hi there," I smiled.

"Hi," she said softly.

"You going to introduce yourself, or what?" Gobbler said with a chuckle.

The girl cleared her throat. "We, uh, already know each other."

"We do?" I said.

She smiled, pressing her lips firmly together. It almost seemed like she was afraid of me. "My name is, uh... Billie... Billie Rae."

It's hard to properly describe shock, but I'll do my best. It hit me like a truck. It knocked the wind out of me. It left me speechless. I was looking at the girl I'd spent three weeks swooning over. I couldn't believe my eyes—literally. I literally thought that I

was imagining the woman in front of me. She was…
beautiful. She was glowing. She had her makeup all
pretty, her hair straightened. She had a pair of white
stockings pulled up her legs.

And I suddenly remembered that she did a
lingerie day each week… so, of course, I was imagining her now in lingerie. I blushed. I cleared my
throat. I squirmed. I made a smile that was probably
very, very lame. "Billie," I said with a squeak in my
voice. "Um, it's, uh, nice to finally meet you in
person."

"Likewise," she said softly.

The terrified look on her face suggested that she
did not want to be seeing me. Maybe she thought
that she was now going to be trapped in a house
with some obsessed freak. All of her stalkers before
were online, messaging her on her various social
media platforms; they were never in the flesh like I
was now. I almost wanted to promise her that I
wouldn't be weird… but words meant nothing. I
would have to prove it with my actions…

But at the same time, she was so beautiful. I
couldn't help but imagine a scenario in which there
was some gamer-house romance between us. I guess
my fantasy was likely her nightmare.

"Look at the two of you," Gobbler said, patting

me hard on the back. "You're like old besties. So, I'm guessing you're our jungler, huh?"

"Yeah," I said. "I guess so." I was red all over. There was a mirror on the back wall letting me know that I looked completely flustered, like a teen boy seeing a girl in a bra for the first time.

"Finally," said Tank. "Gris has been filling in on jungle for the past week. It'll be great to have a pro in the jungle."

"He's good," Billie Rae whispered. She looked at me with a small smile before looking away quickly. I was surprised to see how shy she was. How could a beautiful woman like her be so shy? Did she not stream in underwear? Why did I make her so uncomfortable?

"Have some coffee, J-Rock," said Gobbler, thrusting a mug of black coffee into my hands. "We're going to start grinding in twenty minutes. You get to show us what you can do." He grinned.

I was tense all over. There was so much happening, so fast. And now, Billie Rac's nervous energy was rubbing off on me. I couldn't stop thinking if there was something that I said to her before she left me that last night that we played together. She hadn't spoken to me since then. Did I say something awkward? Did I make her feel scared?

My station was right next to hers. They played a game while I set my computer up. They won quite decisively within twenty-five minutes. "Ready to play, new guy?" Tank asked.

A team could only have five players on it. With eight guys in the house—that made three into alternates. Therefore, we were all competing for a competitive spot. It was how all competitive teams operated. Over the next couple of weeks, we would be competing internally to decide who would get a spot on the main roster.

For me, that meant competition with the one person who was yet to show up at the house. I didn't have to compete with Billie Rae—she specialized in a position called 'mid', and I played a position called 'jungle'. Gobbler played bottom-lane as something called an ADC... look, as I've said before, the game details aren't that important. All you really need to know is, I wasn't an ADC. I wasn't a mid-lane player. I wasn't a support. I wasn't a tank.

Griswold Gamer, the tall, lanky fellow I'd never heard of, was competition for Billie Rae's mid-lane position. Erin (aka Kitten Crusader) was competition for the position as the team's damage-dealer (also known as an ADC) with Gobbler. I would be competing for the role in the jungle. Meanwhile,

Bruce (Tank) was guaranteed a spot as our team's tank, because he was also the team captain—and part of his job was choosing who made the cut and who would sit on the sidelines as an alternate. Roger (aka Race-Star) was our team's only support player, not having to compete with anyone—and that wasn't so controversial, seeing as he was quite possibly the best support player in the country.

So for me, that day should have been relatively relaxing; I wasn't competing for a spot on that roster... yet. It was my chance to get a feel for my new teammates, who would be my teammates for the next few months... and maybe even the next few years.

I'd never played with the same people quite so much. Sure, I'd joined parties before. I'd spent entire nights with the same group of people. Sometimes I played with the same friends night after night... but this was different. These were the best players I'd ever played with, and we all had our roles. Now, instead of going into a game with the simple goal of 'winning', we were going into games with very specific goals in mind: "This time," Bruce, our team captain would say, "I want us all to focus hard on pushing mid-lane. We're going to try to down their mid tower before the five-minute mark."

It was the kind of training I'd always fantasized about, being in that room, with my teammates physically next to me...

But it wasn't going quite as imagined. Now, I was tense. I could smell Billie Rae's perfume. I could see her bare, smooth thighs out of the corner of my eye. Whenever I did something positive for the team, like get an early kill or steal a creep from the enemy jungle, Billie Rae would turn and look at me with a soft smile, those cat-ears perked upright on her headphones. My whole body would tingle, remembering all of those long, personal conversations we'd had before... and that would always lead to me remembering her awkwardly leaving me that one night before ghosting me... Was it something I said? Did she think that I was turning into one of her many stalkers?

Well, now I could see why she had stalkers; she was beautiful. In fact, I would go as far as saying that I'd never seen a more beautiful gamer at a high level like that. Even now, wearing her pyjamas, I was tempted to look at her body. She had the zipper down to her sternum, showing off a bit of her chest. She had small but perky breasts, pushed up in what appeared to be a push-up bra.

She was a distraction, to say the least.

We lost our first game, and it was possibly my fault. When the score sheet came up at the end, there was my name at the very bottom of the list: more deaths than kills, the lowest amount of money and experience gained in the game. I got a nervous glare from our team captain.

Then, Gobbler jumped to his feet and gave me a firm pat on the back. "He's just nervous," he said. "He just needs to get the butterflies out—isn't that right, J-Rock?"

"Sorry guys," I said, blushing. "I'm usually better than that." I looked to Billie Rae for confirmation. She just smiled, but she didn't defend me. I felt suddenly nervous, wondering if maybe I wasn't quite at their level. I started getting terrible thoughts in my head: what if I dragged them down? What if I stopped this team from making it to Nationals?

And then came the replay. Bruce made us sit down and watch the whole thing, from start to finish. It wasn't something I was used to doing... It was tedious, but also humiliating. Everyone in that room had their screen set on me as I relived my blunders. I hardly noticed those blunders during the game... I guess that's the point of watching a replay... but it was horribly awkward, in a room full of strangers, all of them in judgemental model. My first impression had already been set, and it wasn't a good one.

Finally, forty minutes later, it was time for another game. Now, I had to redeem myself. I had to focus on the game, not on what was happening around me...

But it was easier said than done. Now, Billie Rae was out, taking a break while Griswold Gamer took the spot at mid.

We were playing against a random team online, composed of equally ranked players. Griswold was in the zone, leaned close to his screen, determined to be the team's primary mid-lane player... Billie Rae was now painting her fingernails next to me, with her feet up on her desk. She was humming quietly, looking cute... almost as if she was trying to tease me, trying to distract me. Her fluffy onesie was pulled high up her legs, showing more thigh than ever before... and I swear her perfume was even stronger now.

No—that was in my head.

"C'mon, J-Rock!" growled Griswold Gamer. "You need to get those!" Apparently, I missed an easy kill near mid-lane... and that enemy ended up getting a hard hit onto Griswold Gamer, forcing him to retreat while the opposing mid player continued collecting experience and money on that mid-lane.

The game details—as I've said before—aren't important. All you need to know is, Griswold was working hard to do better than Billie Rae, and now, he was already pissed with me, just a few minutes into the game. Because of my blunder, he was playing from behind, grumbling under his breath. And yes, he was clawing his way back into the game with hard work. Around the fifteen-minute mark, I made another little blunder, missing an important attack on an enemy—and that enemy ended up reaching him, killing him as he was trying to escape an ambush. He died. He turned and glared at me, eyes dark, ears fuming. He said nothing… to my face. All of his words were now being grumbled under his breath.

He worked to catch up, now pretending like I wasn't in the game. There were opportunities for us to work together, but he chose to go alone. We could have both gained experience and money from a number of little excursions, but he was convinced I would just weigh him down. Yes, in the end, he did okay. He finished second in kills, behind the opposing team's MVP. We lost, but he still glared at me with a smug smile once it was finished, as if to say, 'I'm better than you, no matter how many times you trip me up.' I sunk into my seat, seeing my name once again at the bottom of that list. Maybe it was my destiny to end up as an alternate.

But I wasn't the one to be scolded by the captain after the game. We watched the replay, and then Bruce turned to Griswold Gamer and shook his head. "This is a team game," he said. "Selfish plays like that are going to cost us important games. You're lucky that wasn't an important game."

I could see Griswold Gamer turning red, about to burst, about to scream in his own defence... but even he knew it wouldn't go well for him, so he kept his trap shut. Then, Bruce turned to me and said, "Keep up the good work." And again, Griswold turned red as he contemplated screaming in his own defence.

It was his turn to sit out. He went off to play games on his own, seemingly determined to prove that he could win games without us. Billie Rae (aka BR-Cat) was back in. She looked at me and smiled.

I was now responsible for two consecutive losses. I really needed to step it up if I was going to keep that spot on that team, that bedroom in that house, and that ticket to my first tournament in more years than I was willing to admit to.

The game started. I was tense, hands trembling. I

focussed hard on making no mistakes. It was another sloppy start, with me getting caught off-guard—not killed, but chased back to the base to heal up, losing precious seconds of grinding time in those early minutes of the game. I saw Griswold glaring over at me, smirking, positive that whoever was coming tonight was going to be replacing me.

I couldn't let him win.

I noticed Billie Rae buying an unusual item—one that she would often buy when we played together before. I knew this strategy of hers. I knew it involved some unorthodox tactics, floating around the map in unexpected ways… unexpected if you weren't familiar with the tactic, that is. I knew this plan, so she didn't even have to ask me to move into position, staying close to her. Her plan was to bait the opponent into thinking she was an easy kill. It was my opportunity to stage an ambush… and it worked. The plan went off perfectly without a word spoken between us. We played well together, thanks to many games playing together.

Now, with their mid-lane player dead, I was able to help her push the tower. We took it down before he respawned: more experience, more money, more of an advantage.

We managed to pull a similar trick a few minutes

later, on the same opponent. "The enemy mid is a total noob," Griswold chimed in from behind us, his jealousy obvious in his voice.

But the enemy mid-lane player was no noob. I recognized his name; he was a frequent player in the top 1500, probably one of the top 300 mid-lane players in the game. If Griswold Gamer had been playing that game for over a decade like me, he would have known that.

We won our first game as a team, and we all cheered as if we'd won a tournament worth a million bucks. Griswold Gamer growled from his corner, now sipping on one of the many free Monster Energy Drinks from one of the many mini-fridges.

And the timing couldn't have been better, as a man stepped into the house, wearing a white dress shirt and freshly ironed tan dress pants. His hair was slicked back. He had a shiny gold Rolex on his wrist. Tank perked up, so we all did the same. "Mr. Tannery," Tank said. "Nice to see you."

"Does that say Victory?" the man, apparently named Mr. Tannery, said.

Tank blushed.

"That's what I like to see," the man said.

Then Tank turned to the rest of us. "Guys, this is

Horatio Tannery. He's the owner of Centennial Greens Cannabis, and the owner of our team."

This was the man who had been contacting me online. He wasn't at all what I expected when I found out he owned a pot shop. I guess it wasn't a strip-mall pot shop… it was a massive chain spanning across Western Canada, and now expanding into the US states where cannabis was legalized.

He took a moment to shake our hands. We all introduced ourselves. Then, he looked at my screen and said, "Looks like you had a good game, John." He looked right into my eyes and smiled. Now, I couldn't see Griswold, but I was sure that he was fuming behind me.

"Thank you, Mr. Tannery," I said.

"Call me Horatio," he said. Then he turned to the rest of the group. "I just wanted to pop in and see how things were shaping up. I booked flights for the qualifiers today. I need to go over some details with Tank. But first, I just want to see how things are going. Maybe you guys could let me watch a game or two." He looked around, spotted the empty chair of the jungler who hadn't yet showed up, and sat down. There was a nervousness in the room, especially with those of us who didn't yet know if we were on the team, or if we were alternates. Tank turned to

better with BR-Cat on mid. Because now, it wasn't about practising tactics; it was about winning.

Griswold stormed off and we didn't see him that night, not even when we gathered with a bottle of champagne to celebrate our 2-1 victory over a well-established team. Bruce was the MPV in both of our wins, and our one loss was a very narrow defeat. We played well together, and that strong victory just cemented Billie Rae as the team's main mid player.

CHAPTER 8

*I*n the night, I heard the newcomer. It must have been close to 3:00 AM, and we'd all only been in bed for an hour, having stayed up to celebrate, polishing off one bottle of champagne, and then a whole case of beer between the seven of us. We all went down tipsy. We all went down with smiles on our faces... well, except, of course, for Griswold Gamer, who spent the night in his own room, playing games on his alternate computer.

The newcomer was quiet, sneaking up to his room, closing the door softly, and then not making another peep. I was nervous. I had no idea who it was, but I had a feeling I would recognize their gamertag... I knew most of the jungle-players in the top 2000… maybe even the top 3000. I was sure he was going to give me a serious run for my money.

But I slept well, half-drunk, exhausted from a long, stressful day. The giddiness of my first streamed victory on a team… it was historic; it was something that I would always remember. I couldn't stop grinning, ear to ear. I must have fallen asleep with a smile on my face.

I was there in the kitchen in the morning, sipping coffee with the rest of them. Even Griswold was there, looking like a new person: calm, collected. He'd had some time to reflect… and apparently, he'd put some serious work into his gaming reputation. While we were partying, he logged an impressive twelve games in the solo-queue, winning eleven, boosting his rank to an impressive 950. Even Bruce's eyes lit up when he saw that we had another team-mate in the top 1000.

Griswold got the first game of the morning while Billie Rae was upstairs, doing her makeup. She was scheduled to stream that night. While we were drinking the night before, she explained to me that part of her contract included three one-hour streams each week. "I can't help but feel like they just brought me in for the publicity," she blushed. She didn't talk much, even when we were drinking. She kept to herself, in her corner. It was so strange to think that somebody who was brave enough to stream in lingerie could be so shy around a small group of nerds. Even after a few beers, she was quiet, blushing whenever someone spoke to her. She didn't get into any one-on-one conversations. I couldn't help but think that my presence was making her ruthlessly uncomfortable. I remembered that last conversation we had, before she started ghosting me. I told her that I wished we could play together in person, and she got awkward and went offline. Now, we were there, together... forced together by forces out of our control...

There was a moment when I thought that I should tap out, leave that team for her sake; maybe that would be the gentlemanly thing to do. But this was my dream; I couldn't just leave because my presence was possibly making a girl uncomfortable.

Griswold won that first game, taking the MVP position. He was beaming now, though he was still doing that thing where he went off on his own. Was he good? Of course. Was he gambling every time he did that? Definitely.

Billie Rae came in for the next game, but wasn't quite herself. She was a bit slugging, maybe with a bit of a hangover. She missed some important shots, lost her tower early, and then found herself scrambling from behind for the rest of the match. It was a lost game. Griswold came in for the next match: another win.

Now, his rank was a glittering 875. He was smiling, beaming, making Billie Rae nervous. She had a pale look on her face. I found her in the kitchen and told her that it was all okay. "I'm just distracted," she said. "I have to do this stream tonight, and I feel like it's just so much to think about right now. I also have to drive to the big city tomorrow for the weekend. There's a lot going on."

"Just relax. You're the better mid," I said. "You'll be just fine. We won that match last night."

She stared into my eyes, looking strangely guilty. I didn't understand that look. I had no idea what it could have meant, so I just smiled and went back to the game room.

Billie Rae was called in. She moved slowly to her computer, logged in, joined the group, and then we joined a game.

It was another rough go: not a terrible game, but not a victory. It wasn't her fault, but she didn't do anything to help either. Griswold didn't gloat, but the grin on his face was obvious. I couldn't blame him; he was clawing his way back onto the team, taking advantage of Billie Rae's bad situation.

Griswold came in, and we won.

Then, it was Billie Rae's turn again. It was going well. We were actually in a decisively lead, with Bruce sitting the game out and Erin taking his spot. Now, Bruce was upstairs, presumably getting himself ready for the day. We took out two towers. We killed three guys without losing one... But then it took a bad turn.

"Wow," a girl voice said behind me. I looked back, not recognizing that voice. Billie Rae and Erin were both in the game with me...

Now, standing behind me was a platinum blonde with a small button nose. She had huge dark eyelashes and a petite body. Her small perky tits weren't in a bra; they didn't need the support, but the lack of bra made it so her nipples were visible through her tight white shirt.

"Don't mind me," she smiled. "Pretend like I'm not here."

"O—Okay," I said, but I could smell her. She was wearing a strong perfume. I swear I could feel the warm heat radiating off of her body.

She was distracting... so I didn't realize that Billie Rae was in the jungle, setting up for one of her classic baits. I wasn't there to help her when the enemy arrived. I was late to rush in, and then she was killed.

I was okay... we were still ahead.

But I missed the next one again. I don't know why, but I just didn't hear her when she told me she was going into the jungle. My mind must have been elsewhere... maybe on the blonde that was now sitting in my peripheral vision. Who was she? Bruce was showing her everything. Was she his girlfriend?

Why was he showing her that empty station? Why was she inspecting the area?

Wait… was she the other jungler?

I looked back. I saw her now with a keyboard. She was setting it up. She must have been the final piece of the team!

It was hard to believe that a girl like that could be a gamer. I mean—yes, Billie Rae was beautiful, and it was hard to believe that Billie Rae was a gamer too… but this was different. I'm not saying that this girl was sexier than Billie Rae; not at all. It was just the way that this girl presented herself: like a Barbie doll, fingers professionally manicured, wearing expensive clothes, with a little purse. Billie Rae had the whole E-girl thing going on. She did her makeup like a classic 'gamer girl'. She wore the E-girl clothes and had gaming tattoos.

"John!" snapped Gobbler. "Can we get a ward down so that doesn't happen again?"

"A ward?" I said. "So what doesn't happen?"

He looked over and glared at me.

I looked at the score and realized we were down. We were losing now—and it was only about to get worse.

I heard Bruce behind me, talking to the girl. "You can play a game or two to warm up. Everyone else will be taking a lunch break soon. Would you prefer I call you Rachael, or Tuesday?"

"Either or," she said with her girly voice.

Wait... Tuesday. There was one jungler in the top 1500 named Tuesday. I'd never played with her... I never even knew that she was a girl. She'd been on a professional team that went to Worlds. In fact, I was pretty sure that she'd won a tournament! I looked back at her. If she had won that tournament, that would explain her expensive fashion.

Then, I looked back, the enemy team was moving in to ambush Billie Rae. "Fuck," I groaned. I tried to make it in time, but I was too late.

Now, the enemy had momentum. They used it to win.

Nobody blamed me for the loss. All eyes went to Billie Rae. She looked to the floor. "Sorry, guys," she said.

"It was my fault," I said, but nobody paid attention to me, because my score was fine. I outplayed the enemy jungler. I had a strong finish, despite the loss. But all the momentum came from Billie Rae's faults... maybe they were my faults. Maybe the game would have gone differently had I been faster to react. Could I blame myself?

"I should probably stop for the day," she said. "I

still have to do that stream… I'm not even close to being ready."

"That was a good game," I said to her. "Minus a few little blips. We'll get the blips smoothed out."

She just smiled at me and then went to get ready for her stream. It was one of her lingerie streams. She had a whole setup in her bedroom; it was the reason she was given the house's master bedroom. Part of her contract included streaming, and she needed that privacy to stream… especially if she was doing it in underwear.

That night, we had another exhibition match with another team, all set up by Bruce. It was streamed. I played jungle while Tuesday watched from behind me. It was a best of three, and we won the first and second round. "You're pretty good," she said to me, batting her big eyelashes.

But the wins weren't because of me. I played average at best, matching the opposing jungler. Bruce was putting up the big numbers, and Griswold played a couple of outstanding games at mid.

Bruce had a bottle of champagne ready. He blushed as he opened it. Then, he looked around, "Where's Billie? Is she still streaming?"

"I think she's getting ready to leave for the weekend," said Erin.

"I'll go see if she wants to come celebrate," I said, perking up at the opportunity to have one last chat with Billie before she left for three days. I wanted to make sure that things between us weren't awkward. The tension was becoming borderline unbearable. She wasn't owning up to any discomfort, but I could tell that there was something there: something making her want to leave that gamer house, never to return.

I went up to her room and saw that the door was half open, so I assumed it was safe to go in. I could hear her packing a bag, so I just pushed the door open and said, "Hey, Billie. We won the tournament, and we were hoping you could come down and—"

She was tense, standing there in a tight orange fishnet one-piece, with nothing covering her breasts underneath. She quickly covered her chest and gasped, and I looked away... a moment too late. Her pussy was covered by black panties, but she still used her other hand to cover her crotch. "John!" she gasped.

I jumped out of the room. "Sorry!" I said. "Your door was open, and... I thought you were packing!"

"I am packing!" she said. "I was just out using the bathroom! The door didn't close all the way! That doesn't mean that you can just let yourself in!"

"I'm sorry!" I gasped.

I knew that my face was dark red. I knew that I hadn't made anything better with the blunder; now, if there was tension before, it was only going to get worse.

There was a long silence before she said, "Okay, come in."

Now, she had a grey satin kimono over her lingerie-clad body. Her cheeks were dark red and her gaze was turned to the floor. "What did you want?"

Again, I invited her downstairs, but she declined the offer. "I have to pack to go. I can't have a drink before driving down the freeway."

"You could just hang out for a bit."

I looked at her bags. They were all packed. Was she leaving for good? "You're coming back... right?"

"I just have to deal with some things back home," she said.

"I know today was a bit of a bust, but that doesn't mean you're off the team, Billie. Griswold had a good day. But you're the better jungler. Believe me; you're way easier to play with. Don't leave. Okay?"

She made a small smile. "You're sweet, John," she said. "I'm not worried about that. It's… It's just personal stuff that I have to square up."

"Okay," I said. Then I smiled. "I'm looking forward to training with you when you're back."

She stared into my eyes for a long moment… a long, long moment. Why was she still staring into my eyes? Why wasn't she looking away? Did she have something to say? Was she waiting for me to leave? "John, can you, uh, close that door?"

I closed the door. My heart fluttered. Was she going to address the awkward elephant in the room now? Was she going to bring up that terrible final moment we had together before she ghosted me? "What is it?" I asked.

"There's something that I should probably come clean about. I—I don't really know how to say this, and I feel like you're going to get really weird about it…"

"What is it?" I asked. Now, my heart was racing. Was she going to tell me that she had a boyfriend, and her boyfriend didn't know that we played together or something?

She kept staring into my eyes, afraid to say anything. "Promise to keep it a secret?"

"Sure. Whatever," I said.

She turned that gaze to the floor. "Griswold doesn't know it, but he's going to be the mid alternate."

"What?" I said. "What makes you say that? I mean —I know you're the better player on mid. But… How can you be so confident."

"I'm not the better player," she said. "He's really good. But… He's just here while I square things off back home. Bruce doesn't even know it. I talked about it with Horatio. Part of my contract is that I'm guaranteed a spot on the main roster as long as I'm streaming: three times a week now, and then five times once the circuit starts. It's part of the sponsorship endorsement with Centennial Greens."

"Wait… actually?" I said.

She nodded her head, looking guilty. "He's just filling in while I go back and forth. I might have to miss an important game or two in the pre-season—maybe early in the National circuit season. He'll fill in for me, and then he'll just be an alternate. We don't have Centennial Greens as a sponsor without me on the main roster. It's been weighing on me, John. It's really not something I'm happy about, but they want me and Bruce to be like the faces of the team: he's the veteran gamer that everyone knows, and I'm the fresh streamer with the big following."

"I—I guess that makes sense."

"But we can't lose our pre-season matches. We need a pro mid to fill in, and nobody would agree to doing it knowing they're just temporary." She looked down again. "Please don't tell anyone."

"It's fine. Your secret is safe with me," I said. "But, uh, he's going to be mad."

"He's not going to find out," she said, darting her

gaze up to look into my eyes. "I just… I need to play better, so he doesn't get too suspicious when Bruce names me as the main. Ideally, Horatio won't even have to tell Bruce to pick me over him; the goal is that it happens naturally. But after today…"

"Today was just a hiccup," I said. "We all have bad days. Franklin's bad day was yesterday. And honestly, he played fine today, but he's still being selfish, making risky plays. You can't play like that in a tournament. Bruce would never take the risk."

She let out a small smile. "I'm glad you're here, John," she said softly. "I really missed playing with you."

"And I'm glad you're here," I smiled. "I really thought I would come here and it would be a bunch of guys with bad B.O. It's nice to have a pretty girl here."

She blushed, and then I blushed harder.

"Sorry," I said. "I'm not hitting on you. But, uh, you are pretty. You're really pretty. And, uh, it's honestly been distracting. I hope I'm not making you feel uncomfortable. I'm not trying to. I just… I just want you to know, I guess… I don't know why." I knew that I was starting to ramble, and it only got worse from there. Honestly, I can't even remember what I said after that, but I went on for another embarrassing minute, rambling on and on, trying to dig myself out of a hole while only putting myself deeper into it. She finally shut me up by walking up to me and giving me a kiss on the lips. It was a beautiful five-second kiss that ended with her pulling her head away and saying, "I'm sorry, I don't know why I did that."

And how could I control myself after that? How could I keep my hands off of her? I grabbed her and threw her onto her bed. She laughed, her body bouncing playfully. I pounced onto her and pushed her arms up, over her head. I looked down into her glittering eyes. She turned red, letting out a pretty little gasp.

I knew this was a big mistake. I knew this was only going to complicate an already complicated situation… and I really had no idea just how complicated I was about to make her situation, and my situation. But now, it seemed like the damage had been done; I had nothing left to lose, so I went in for another kiss, and she accepted it.

I could feel some reluctance. She was a shy girl, no matter how she presented herself. It was a minute before she finally parted her lips enough to share tongues. When I moved my hands on her body, she grabbed my wrists to stop them. I caught myself tempted to apologize a few times, but I didn't want to kill the mood. She was warming up... slowly. She would close her eyes, take a slow breath, and then she would allow it to go a little bit further.

"They're going to wonder where we are," I whispered.

"Then you better be fast," she said.

I felt her hand reaching down into my pants. I felt her fingers wrapping around my erection. I gasped as she began to tug. I watched her face flush red. I watched her eyes glitter. "Oh my God," I heard her whisper. "It's... hard."

"Why are you surprised?" I asked with a nervous little laugh.

In that moment, I felt like my dreams had finally come true in every way imaginable: all of that hard work, all of that suffering... it was all finally paying off. I was on a pro team. I was living in a gamer house. I basically had a girlfriend now too: a smoking hot E-girl girlfriend: every gamer boy's dreams.

But the ultimate fantasy was about to hit its first big bump in the road. "Before we go any further, I should, uh, tell you something else."

"What is it?" I asked.

She blinked a few times. She blushed and smiled nervously. "I was, uh, born a boy."

Remember when I tried to describe what it felt like to be truly shocked? Well... I thought I knew before... Now, I was experiencing it all over again with twice the intensity. Now, I really got to feel the force a dump truck ramming me in the chest, knocking the air out of my lungs. There was hardly a moment of questioning her, because she showed me by motioning down. There it was: Hard, out from her panties, squished into that fishnet outfit, but still undeniably real.

But I wasn't one to judge. Born a boy or not, she was hot. She was cute. She was fun to be around. "I never liked kids much anyway," I said, and then we went back at it. We kissed, tongue and all, moving ahead like we were in a rush... because we were in a rush. We pushed our bodies hard together. I felt her erection against mine. I thought I was going to end up inside of her, and then she reached down, grabbed her cock, and she pulled her tip to my hole. "I've never done this," I warned her, tensing up.

"We can take turns," she said, and a moment later, she was inside of me. I was scrambling for something to hold onto. I gasped loudly, and she covered my mouth with the palm of her hand so that our housemates wouldn't hear us. But that didn't stop her from pushing her long nine-inch shaft deep into my body.

My eyes rolled into the back of my head. I trembled all over. I wondered if I was making a huge mistake, and then I looked at her face and saw how beautiful she was, and I pushed that worry away. She began to thrust up into me. I grabbed her breasts and held firmly, like a child riding a horse for the first time, terrified I was going to be bucked off.

She used every inch, and she didn't last long: a minute of thrusting, ending with a warm gushing deep inside of me. I moaned and went limp, so she took control. She reached down, took my erection, and stuffed it into her own hole. She began to push herself against me, and soon, I had the strength to take over, fucking her for a minute until I was gushing inside of her.

I was pulsing all over with pleasure that I'd never experienced before. I looked into her face and saw the most beautiful shade of glowing pink. I had a feeling that I was going to like living in the house. It just felt like all of the pieces of my life were finally falling into place.

I remembered that my housemates were downstairs, probably starting to wonder where I went. I'd been gone for twenty minutes. Not wanting them to think that there was anything happening between me and Billie Rae, I quickly thanked her for the fun and slipped downstairs. I assumed I would see her again before she left, but she managed to sneak away unnoticed through the back door while we were all enjoying our celebration. Nobody noticed her leaving—especially not Franklin (aka Griswold Gamer), because he was a completely different person: beaming, smiling, boisterous… and drunk. He even started singing, and got everyone to sing along (it was some popular Journey song or another… it's hard to remember, because I had a couple of drinks myself).

Seeing him with such a grand smile on his face filled me with a taste of the guilt and dread that Billie Rae must have been feeling. So I went up to see how she was doing, and that's when I noticed that she was gone.

CHAPTER 9

*T*here were no days off in the Red Deer team house. We all wanted to win, and we knew that meant daily work… and this wasn't the fun kind of gaming that most people think about when they talk about playing video games. We had a rigid structure. Bruce had us practising drills, working on muscle memory. That Saturday, he had me working on perfecting a very specific sequence of skills, which involved me hitting nine different keys on the keyboard in perfect succession while also clicking on a moving target on the screen. He didn't let me stop until I could do it seamlessly thirty times in a row—and fast, in under 1.5 seconds.

And that was just one drill. That was only going to prove useful if I ended up playing with that specific hero (and there were hundreds in the game), and only if I ended up getting all those specific items and putting my skill points into those specific skills. It was something that would probably only come in handy in 5% of the games we played... but that was the difference between being in the top 2,000 and being in the top 200.

Griswold Gamer was finding his groove.

Bruce sat down with him on Sunday to discuss his selfish play style. They had a chat for over an hour before coming back down to return to playing with us. Franklin looked a bit stunned: white skin and red eyes, as if he'd been close to tears during the talk. I wondered if Bruce broke the news to him: that Billie Rae would be the main mid player… but now, Franklin was modifying his game. I was shocked when he said to me, "J-Rock, let's take out their jungler when he goes by my ward." I'm not sure he'd ever communicated with me directly like that.

Together, we got their jungler. Now, we were starting to jive. We were winning game after game. My rank was now 1,200: the highest it had ever been.

Tuesday subbed into the jungle and I sat out, taking a rare break. Tuesday was good… but not professional team good. I was fairly confident that she wouldn't be much competition. We would even play five-on-five scrimmages, getting Bruce's pro player friends to sub into the empty spots so we could play without affecting our ranks. I got to play against Tuesday in those scrims, and I outplayed her consistently.

She was past her gaming prime. And it seemed as though she was just happy to be in the house, playing every day—even if it just meant being an alternate. I suppose I would have been perfectly happy being an alternate; alternates still got to share the prize money, whether or not they played. They were important pieces of the team, and she was providing an invaluable service during those scrims. Bruce would tell her in secret what strategies to use, and he would see how I responded.

We were all improving quickly. We were getting better at playing together—and it became quickly obvious when we were matched with a team ranked in the 1,500-2,000 range. We stomped them ruthlessly, as if they were little kids playing their first ever game. It was already starting to seem crazy that I was ever in that rank range.

After playing that game for twelve years, I really didn't think that I had anything left to learn; I thought that I was just a lower rank than the top guys because they had faster reflexes and better luck... but now I was seeing that I could be so much better.

Tuesday came into my room on that Sunday night. She had a big smile on her face. "Hi John!" she said with her cutesy voice. She stepped in and carefully closed the door behind her, insinuating she wanted to have a private conversation.

"What's up, Tues?" I smiled.

"I just wanted to, uh, congratulate you on your big win streak." She blushed as she looked at me. I can honestly say that no girl had ever looked at me like that before—and definitely not a beautiful woman who could have easily had a career as a model. I felt suddenly star-struck, blushing all over, remembering that she had achieved heights that I could only dream of. She'd been on tournament circuits. She'd held up trophies and cashed cheques worth nearly a quarter-million dollars. She knew the limelight that I fantasized on a nightly basis.

"Thanks," I said. "I've been on a lucky streak."

"It's not luck," she said. "You're good. I watched the replay from your last game. The way that you knew to skirt around those enemy wards... I would never think to play like that. It's just so... smart!"

I was dark red now, grinning like a fool. "Thanks, Tues. You're not so bad yourself."

She giggled. "I'm past my prime," she said. "I'm just happy to be here. I missed it. You know, it's been three years since I've been on a team like this."

"Has it been that long?" I said. "I can still remember when you were playing with Fox Gaming. That was... iconic."

Now she was blushing. My heart was racing as I discovered I could make a girl like her blush. Female attention was not something that I was used to. I'd never considered myself particularly handsome... And I had never had money or any achievements that might make a skirt wet. Now, I still wasn't particularly handsome, and I still didn't have any money... but in the world of professional gaming, I was someone.

"Did you hear about the interviews?" she asked.

"Interviews?" I said.

"Bruce sent out an email to our team addresses. E-Sports Daily is coming to interview all of us on Wednesday. That's exciting, huh?"

"Totally," I said.

But she wasn't leaving. She was standing there, smiling, waiting to say something else. Finally, she giggled and opened the door. "Sorry, John. I didn't mean to bother you."

"It wasn't any bother at all," I blushed.

She giggled again. "You're cute," she said casually before skipping off. Now, my heart was fluttering. Was she... hitting on me? Was she interested in me?

I suddenly thought of my romp with Billie Rae. She probably left the house with feelings for me... feelings that were probably developing with her time away from me. My feelings had been developing for her too. I'd been fantasizing frequently about going down on her, sucking her off and making her cum in my mouth. I'd been dreaming of bending her over and filling her ass with my seed...

But Billie Rae seemed... complicated. Her

shyness made her mysterious, and her situation with her streaming contract... and the fact that she would stream in lingerie, flirting with her viewers. She knew how to use her sexuality to win over an audience, and maybe she was using it to win me onto her side as well. She knew that the situation with Griswold Gamer was going to be complicated, possibly causing a rift in the house, and she surely knew that I would now be on her side, no matter what.

She came in late that night, while most of us were still awake. We'd just finished a two-hour break, and now we were gaming again, experimenting with the newest game patch that changed the stats of many heroes in the game developers's attempt to balance the game more evenly (it wasn't something that I would have normally paid much attention to, but Bruce was fierce when it came to the small details).

I turned and smiled at Billie Rae before turning back to the game. She returned the smile quickly before scurrying up to her bedroom. I didn't see her again that night. Her room was dark and she was presumably asleep by the time we finished training for the night. I was excited to see her in the morning...

And it was well worth the wait. Now, she was

CHAPTER 10

For weeks, Billie Rae and I snuck off to fuck in the various rooms of that gamer house. It seemed like every conversation we had would end in us going at it like animals. Soon, I was starting to think of it as something more serious than just gamers with benefits. I started fantasizing about more: a real relationship as boyfriend and girlfriend. Sure, we would have to keep it secret until we could have a serious discussion with Bruce about it.

But when I tried to take things further with Billie Rae, I was stone-walled. I asked her more personal questions, questions about her past, about her childhood. She just went silent. She would look away, and then I would find myself apologizing, even though the questions seemed totally innocent, like, "What city did you grow up in?" She just didn't want to tell me anything about her past. She only wanted to talk about the present.

It just made her seem more complicated... and it also made it seem like she was hiding something— something even bigger than the drama with Griswold Gamer.

I did take her downstairs late one night to practise with her while the others slept. I wanted her to be better than Griswold Gamer, to avoid a complete catastrophe... and it helped a little bit. She seemed to be finding her game again. She started winning more consistently, putting up better numbers. She seemed to be in a calmer headspace.

But it just wasn't enough. Griswold Gamer reached 455 rank. He was one of the top 100 mid-lane players in the game. He was the obvious choice for mid-lane. And Bruce was constantly patting him on the back, and putting him into our streamed exhibition games...

Then, Horatio from Centennial Greens came to the house. He took Bruce upstairs. They were up there for a long time. I could feel the energy in the house changing. I could feel a storm of dark, negativity flooding into the house. Horatio came downstairs and left without speaking to anyone else. Bruce came down five minutes later. He called Griswold Gamer to follow him upstairs. Ten minutes later, Griswold Gamer was storming out of the house, suitcase packed and in hand. He left without saying anything to anyone. Bruce tried to stop him. "Let's talk about this, Franklin," he called out from the door.

Then, Franklin stopped and turned to face Bruce from the front lawn. "You'll be lucky if I don't sue you're shit team!" And then he got into his car and left.

An awful silence came over the house. Then, Tuesday asked, "What just happened?"

"I gave main jungler to BR-Cat for the tournament this weekend," he said, looking at the ground. "Griswold was just too much of a loose cannon. His play style was too unpredictable. And if this is how he's going to act whenever he doesn't get his way, then, uh, I guess we'll be bringing in a new player to fill out the roster."

I knew the truth. I knew that that Horatio came and told Bruce that he had to choose Billie Rae. Maybe he didn't give the full reason, but it wasn't presented to Bruce as an option.

Later that evening, Bruce took me upstairs to let me know I would be the starter in jungle for the qualifier. "Tuesday will sit out as alternate. If you play strong, we'll keep you in for all the games. Okay?"

I smiled. I was beaming with pride... and it should have been the proudest moment of my life... but the drama between Griswold Gamer and Billie Rae overshadowed the moment. It was weighing on everyone. It wasn't long before players started whispering. I was in the kitchen when Gobbler nodded for me to approach him. "You think Billie Rae is fucking Bruce?" he asked me.

"What? Why?"

"I mean... come on. Franklin is one of the top mids in the world. We all know it."

"As of recently," I said. "Two weeks ago, he was hardly in the top 1,500. Bruce is right: Franklin is unpredictable."

"It's just weird to me," said Gobbler. "That's all I'm saying."

But I knew that little rumour was getting around. I even overheard Gobbler suggesting to Race-Star that Billie Rae had slept with Horatio. And how could I blame the men for coming to that conclusion? The truth is: we would have probably been a better team with Griswold Gamer at mid...

I still had high hopes for Billie Rae. When she was playing at the top of her game, she was unbeatable. She was, quite possibly, the best active female in the game. I wanted her to prove everyone wrong.

But going into that tournament, she certainly was not playing the best League of Legends of her life.

It was Thursday evening when we boarded that plane, tickets paid for by Centennial Greens. Horatio was there with us, clad in a fitted suit, expensive watch, slicked back hair. He was wearing sunglasses, as if he was expecting paparazzi. Were we expecting paparazzi?

MONTREAL, QUEBEC: CANADIAN E-SPORTS NATIONAL QUALIFIERS

There were cameramen at the airport: a dozen of them, spotting us and rushing towards us. They started shooting off questions. Bruce stepped forward to let them all know that the press conference wasn't until the morning.

My heart was racing. I looked over at Tuesday, who was quickly touching up her pink lip gloss. She was beaming, red in the cheeks, excited to get another taste of the stardom that she once had. Billie Rae was the opposite, stepping back and turning her chin down… but that didn't stop the paparazzi from circling around to get photos of her. In fact, it seemed like they wanted photos of her and nobody else.

"Can you comment on social media posts made by your former member, Griswold Gamer?" one reporter shouted.

I knew that the game had been growing in popularity with each passing year, but I didn't realize people cared his much. People in the airport saw the media swarm and moved in to see if we were famous. Amazingly, someone recognized Bruce and shouted out to him. That same person recognized Billie Rae and shouted to her. They both waved: Bruce with a charming smile, Billie Rae with a nervous, shy glare.

Our hotel rooms were booked by Centennial Greens. We were given four rooms, each with a pair of queen-sized beds. It was a nice hotel, less than a block from the convention centre where the three-day tournament was being held. Bruce and Gobbler got right to setting up our towers so we could do some last-minute training.

I was put into a room with Race-Star. Erin

bunked up with Billie Rae, and Tuesday got her own room.

After nearly a month with the team, Race-Star (whose real name was Roger), was probably the one person I hardly knew at all. He was a chatty guy… with everyone else. But when he was with me, he would just go silent, and I would do the same. You know when you just don't quite jive with a person? It's not like I had anything against him or that he had anything against me… we just didn't have that connection. Maybe it was something astrological…

"Excited?" he asked me, trying to break the silence between us as we unpacked our gear.

"That's an understatement," I said.

"This is your first tournament, right?"

I nodded my head, a bit embarrassed to admit it, seeing as I was the oldest on the team.

"You'll be fine," he said. "Just try to get the jitters out quickly. If we lose three round-robin matches, we're eliminated." I don't know why he was telling me that.

"I know," I said. It was my first tournament, but I still knew how tournaments worked. I knew that there were five round-robin matches (all best of three), and I knew that the scores from the round-robin were used to seed the quarter-finals. I knew that the top team in the round-robin round got a pass through quarters, straight to semis. Simply put, only the top seven teams advanced past the round-robin stage, and there were fifteen teams in the tournament.

I wasn't too worried. We had Bruce, and he was one of the best players in the entire country. We had Roger, who was a fierce competitor. We had Gobbler, who was well-known in the gaming community as being extremely consistent.

But then there was Billie Rae, playing one of the most important positions. It didn't matter how good the rest of us were; if we were slaughtered in the middle lane, there was no way to win…

As the jungler, it's your job to float around the map. The other players all have their lanes that they stick to for a large chunk of the game; that's where they gain their money and experience. But the junglers move around, in the jungle, from lane to lane, into the enemy side of the map… a jungler needs to be versatile and extremely aware of what's happening all over the game map. But with Billie Rae's recent inconsistence, I felt like I was going to need to play near that middle lane at all times, ready to help her whenever she needed help… and that meant neglecting the other teammates. Billie Rae's rough patch affected me more than anyone else on the team.

"Do you like her?" Race-Star asked me suddenly, as I was pulling my nightwear out from my suitcase.

"Like her?" I said.

"I saw you with her the other night," he said with a little grin. "Not to be that guy, but there is a rule against relationships in the house."

My heart skipped a beat. I could feel myself turning pale. Did he see me with Billie Rae? Did he see us fucking? We'd snuck downstairs in the night together, a few nights earlier, and fucked in the kitchen. I was sure that I heard someone there... I even stopped ramming her to listen, but she was certain it was just the house settling. Now, I was even less sure.

"She's hot, man," he continued. "But remember that we have to remain professional. I've seen things get complicated before. That's what ruined Team Ivy."

I stuttered. I was about to defend myself, and then he said, "I can't blame you though. Her blonde hair... Oh man. I've always had a thing for blondes. And honestly, you're a lot better than her in the jungle—between you and me. I can see her leaving the team in a few months—somewhere she won't have to just be an alternate."

And I realized he was talking about Tuesday.

"I don't have anything going on with Tuesday," I said. "I'm not sure what you think you saw."

He grinned. "You were just really close. She was playing with her hair and you guys were chatting… for like thirty straight minutes. Hey man—like I said: I don't blame you. She's hot. I used to have a picture of her as my desktop background. I just feel like it's my duty as your teammate to remind you to keep it professional."

"Of course," I said. "Don't worry about that at all."

CHAPTER 11

I will try to keep the details of that day short, as they aren't terribly relevant to the story, but I feel the need to describe the amazing sights and sounds regardless. When we arrived, the place was already packed with fans. There was a line down the street to get in. Stands had been set up in a huge semi-circle around the main stage, with five computers facing five computers, divided by a plexiglass wall so teams couldn't eavesdrop on one another.

There were lights shining down on that stage. Crews were testing those lighting setups: flashing lights, neon lights, spotlights... Theatre-sized screens were up to show the game, where players couldn't see them. In the heavens of the convention centre were floating booths, filled with broadcasters, streaming in five different languages. One of the massive screens was showing the main feed, which was already being streamed live—already with 100,000 viewers tuned in, and the first match was still an hour away.

We had our badges on lanyards around our necks. Seat-holders had black lanyards and we had red ones. Everyone stopped and gawked at anyone wearing a red lanyard. I made the mistake of going through the main lobby, just to see the action from the other side, and I was quickly swarmed with people who called themselves fans. They wanted signatures. They wanted pictures. I was like a celebrity. I'm not sure if they actually knew who I was, or if I was just the closest person with a red lanyard.

They wished me luck. They told me they loved me. One girl looked into my eyes and, without hesitating, asked if I was single.

I was red all over. It was an ego overload. I tried not to let it get to my head. I knew that I hadn't achieved anything until I had an achievement to show for it. If we didn't take one of the top three spots (meaning we either had to qualify for the A-final, or win the B-final), then we weren't going to be going to Nationals. Three teams already has passes to Nationals, so they weren't there that weekend... but they were surely watching from home, taking notes, sizing up their competition.

But enough about that. We were all whisked away to the press conference. We sat up on a stage for twenty minutes and asked questions while being blinded by constant flash-photography. Many of the reporters asked about me. They wanted to know how long I'd been playing, and why I hadn't made any professional appearances before. "I never really took it seriously until recently," I blushed.

Soon, the questions were onto Bruce and Billie Rae. The big controversy of the Canadian gaming world: why was Billie Rae given the main spot? It was during that press conference that we learned Griswold Gamer had already done a press conference, answering a set of similar questions... because he was competing. "He's here?" Bruce asked.

"He was recruited to Team Horizon two days ago," said a reporter.

We all fell silent. This was horrible news—in part because Griswold Gamer was one of the best mid-lane players in the world and knew Billie Rae's play style more than any other player in that tournament —and in part because his presence there alone was enough to put Billie Rae back into that state of terror, guilt, and flustered confusion. When she was like that, she did not play her best League of Legends...

And our first game of the day was against the HGA: The Horizon Gaming Association. Griswold glared at us with a dark look in his eyes as he took to the stage. Billie Rae seemed to freeze. Her mind was suddenly elsewhere. You see, there's a stage in competitive League of Legends where each player gets an allotted time to pick their character. When it was Billie Rae's turn, she just sat there, not making a choice. Gobbler had to reach over and nudge her out of her state of hypnosis. "You have twenty seconds left. Why aren't you choosing?" he said into his headset.

I believe this was what they call a 'worst case scenario'. It set a bad tone for the competition.

We lost in just twenty-four minutes. And just for reference, a normal game usually goes longer than forty-five minutes.

Billie Rae was sadly to blame for the loss. I tried to cover her, but she kept making the same blunders, even letting herself be killed by the creeps near the beginning of the match.

It was a best of three... but game two went just as badly as game one. Let's not even talk about game two...

Bruce was dead-silent after the games

"There are still lots of games today," Gobbler said, trying to improve the mood. But one big opportunity was already gone... the top team got to skip the quarter final round, and the top team almost always went 5-0 in the round-robin. Now, for us, that was an impossibility.

I took Billie Rae aside and put my hands on her shoulders. "You okay?" I asked.

She smiled. "I'm fine," she said. "I just... I didn't expect quite so much press."

For the next game, she came out wearing a baseball cap under her cat-ear headset. It almost seemed like she was trying to hide her face.

"Okay, guys," Bruce said before the start of the match. "This is an easy one for us. This should be a freebie." And it was true: Millennium Gaming was, by far, the worst team in the contest, with a couple of players not even ranked in the top 10,000. Their acceptance into the tournament was a complete mystery, and they were completely stomped (like us) in their first match.

But beating them wasn't as easy as we thought. It was going well at first, and then Billie Rae made a fatal mistake, not being aware of the enemy on the map. She walked right into them, giving them that free kill... And worse, she was doing something called 'pulling a camp'. It was, honestly, something she shouldn't have been doing in that moment—and now, she not only gave up herself, she gave up that camp. When you kill a special camp in the game, you get a temporary buff to your stats. The enemy used that temporary buff to take out a tower, to kill Bruce who tried to save the tower, and then to push up into our territory—just enough that they now had the momentum.

I won't bore you with game details. Long story short: we were playing from behind after that, and we just never caught up. We lost. And then we lost again, closing out that best-of-three.

We were 0-2 now. One more loss and that was it for us: no quarter finals, no Nationals, no Worlds. It would probably mean a rejigging of the roster for next year... if Centennial Greens even wanted to pursue another year, or if this would be chalked up as a failed experiment.

Billie Rae went to get some fresh air after the game. Bruce waved Tuesday over and talked quietly to her, away from the rest of us—but we all knew what he was saying... He was asking her if she would consider stepping into that mid spot.

Tuesday was a jungler, like me. But she had experience playing other roles. And right now, it seemed like anyone would be better than Billie Rae at mid.

We had one hour before our third match—and we had to win that match. Bruce had a big decision to make. He had two potential replacements for Billie-Rae: Tuesday and Kitten Krusader. Neither were mid specialists, but both knew the game well enough to fill in on mid in a pinch. Bruce went to Gobbler, pulling him aside. They chatted for a few minutes. Then he went to Race-Star. They chatted for ten long minutes. Now, Billie Rae was back, so Bruce was having these conversations far away, in another area of the convention centre.

Finally, he came to me. "John, can I talk to you for a minute?"

I followed him up the stairs, to the staff area of the centre, near the hallway that led to the broad-casting booths. "What is it?" I asked, even though I knew exactly what it was.

"Billie Rae isn't playing at the top of her game," he

said. "I—I don't really know what to do right now. I'm in a bit of a bind."

I was silent, tense all over. This wasn't how I wanted my pro gaming career to end: going 0-3 in the round-robin of a qualifier tournament. I knew that it was true: Billie Rae was bombing. In fact, during that break, they were showing individual stats on the main screen: stats from the first two rounds of round-robin. Down, near the very, very bottom of that long, long list—seventy-nine players who had played in at least one game so far—was Billie Rae. There were only two players lower than her, with more deaths and fewer kills. "A team is only as strong as its weakest link," Bruce said.

I cleared my throat. "She had a rough couple of games, but I don't think she's our weakest link. I—I should have been there to help her during that ambush at the start of the last game."

"You were helping at top," Bruce said. "That's where you were supposed to be. Don't try to take the blame, John. Those losses weren't your fault. Right now, we need to win our next three rounds, or we're out."

I felt cold all over.

"Anyway," Bruce said. "I've spoken to the whole team. I'm taking a vote. I'm not voting myself; I'm putting it up to the rest of you. Right now, it's a split decision. You have to be our tie-breaker."

"Me!?" I said.

"Her performance at mid affects you as our jungler more than anyone else. It has to be your choice. Who would you prefer to have at mid? Tuesday, Kitten, or Billie Rae?"

I could feel myself turning white. Why was this being put on me? "You're the captain, Bruce. You have to pick," I said.

"I can't pick," he said, tensing up. He stuttered for a moment, but he said nothing else. I knew what he was saying: he had been ordered by Horatio to keep Billie Rae on the roster... but if the rest of us voted to swap her out, that was a different story. It was a loophole in the agreement, because the rest of us didn't know about Billie Rae's contract with Centennial Greens—as far as Bruce knew. "I need you to pick."

He stared into my eyes. If my theory was right, and he was trying to use me as a loophole to oust Billie Rae for the rest of the tournament, then that meant he was probably hoping I would suggest giving her the boot...

But I couldn't do it. I couldn't crush Billie Rae like that. Maybe my feelings were getting in the way of my judgement… "We'll leave Billie Rae in," I said. "I think she'll do better next game."

He stared at me, wide-eyed and pale-faced. There was a tense silence, and for a moment, his eyes seemed to say, 'If she fucks up, you're the one being cut.' My heart fluttered down into the pit of my stomach. I tried to force a smile. "It'll be fine," I said.

But it wasn't looking so fine. We were up against Force-Five Gaming, the previous year's National champions. They were 2-0 in their first two bouts, one win away from securing a spot in the quarter finals.

We were up in three matches: lots of time to

marinade in our awful state of anxiety. We were all silent: sitting, waiting…

We didn't speak… we just waited. And it didn't feel like we were waiting for our next game; it felt like we were waiting for our *final* game.

CHAPTER 12

*B*illie Rae was sitting right next to me. Her face was pale and her eyes were red. She'd been crying, overwhelmed with the guilt of putting the team through this. It was about to be her fault that the seven of us would be sitting the rest of the year out, possibly never to play professionally again.

She looked over at me slowly during the character selection screen. She blinked a few times. I noticed her hands trembling. "Relax," I said. "You've got this. Alright?"

She forced a small smile and then she wiped her eyes.

"I'm going to have your back out there," I continued. "We'll be fine."

She nodded her head slowly. I saw her take a deep breath. The pressure really was on. She didn't just have to pull through for that game; we had to win that whole best-of-three... and then the next best-of-three, and then the one after that too. Oh, and that wasn't all. We also had to win our quarter final match. If we wón all of those games, we had a fifty-percent chance at qualifying.

"One game at a time," Bruce whispered into his mic. I think he was talking to himself.

I hate to say it, but Billie Rae's game did not improve. She was, once again, the first one to die, giving up valuable experience to their mid-lane player. I looked over and saw some seriously pale faces in our group. Billie Rae didn't make eye-contact with any of us, too ashamed.

And she didn't improve from there. She gave up another kill before becoming increasingly cautious... overly cautious, hiding behind her tower until it went down, and then she retreated into our jungle to 'farm creeps'. I've said it a thousand times: the game details really aren't important, as long as you understand that she was not helping us to win...

But we did win—not because of Billie Rae, but because Bruce went for a super aggressive strategy, buying risky items and making risky moves to attack the enemy. He got lucky a couple of times; the enemy thought they had us pinned, so they didn't bother to purchase wards to place around their own end of the playing field. Bruce, a League of Legends genius, used this to his advantage, slipping into the enemy jungle and picking off enemies as they tried to pass through. He killed three of them before they decided to buy the wards, but now, he was powerful. While they were scrambling to ward their jungle, he pushed a tower and destroyed it. He escaped untouched and then he pushed the mid-lane tower while the rest of us were defending an enemy push up top. He became even more powerful and commanded Billie Rae to stay back, close to our base, where she wouldn't be able to 'feed' the enemy. Billie Rae was embarrassed, red all over, but we ended up winning.

In the next game, I saved her from nearly being the first death of the game. I picked my champion based on the knowledge that it would be my job to keep her safe. Now, the enemy team knew that she was our weak link, so they were targeting her; that was a big mistake, because it made them predictable. When they went to kill her, I was ready, jumping in, snaring the enemy right next to our tower. The tower targeting the enemy and killed him.

I would have normally upgraded my strength with the money from the kill, but I knew they would be back for Billie Rae, so I bought wards, to get visibility on their end. I hid them in their jungle, and those wards showed us when the enemy was coming back, trying to ambush Billie Rae. Bruce came down when he saw their little red dots on his mini-map. He was ready for them, and I was there to snare them so Bruce could smash them to pieces.

We won that game easily, but again, Billie Rae wasn't the reason we won.

And nobody on the team was relaxed yet. We were 1-2, still with two matchups left; we had to win both.

Billie Rae went for a walk. I watched her, hands buried into the pockets of her hoodie. She went down a narrow hallway that went to some storage closets, and I decided to follow her. I found her crying, in the nook of a locked doorway. She looked up at me and turned her face away quickly. "What's the matter?" I asked.

"You know," she said. "I shouldn't be here. This is just… embarrassing. I'm completely out of my league."

"You're doing fine. Are you playing your best? No

—but you're doing fine. You shouldn't be so hard on yourself."

"I'm at the bottom of the list, John," she said. "I'm letting you all down. I—I should just drop out."

"Please don't," I said. "This is your dream. You're being too hard on yourself."

"It's your dream too," she said, looking up into my eyes. She paused for a moment, letting her comment sink in. And it really did hit me in a powerful way: she was right, this was my dream, and if we lost because of her... then my dream would be over... because of her.

I bit down on my tongue and took a deep breath. I knew that she was capable of more. I'd played with her when she was totally dominant. I'd seen her outplay Griswold Gamer, who was the top rated mid player in that building. "I want to play with you," I said. "Please don't drop out."

She stared into my eyes for a moment longer.

"Everyone voted," she said. "I know because Erin told me. Bruce asked her to vote. You voted for me to stay in, didn't you?"

I blushed and shrugged my shoulders.

"You didn't have to do that for me, John. You don't have to put me before your own interests."

"I made my choice," I said. "And I'm sticking to it. I want you to play."

She blushed harder, biting her lip, looking away. Then, she peeked down the hallway. She grabbed my wrist and pulled me into the nook of that doorway, far away from the noise of that convention centre. Next, she shimmied her pants down, exposing her panties. She put a hand on my shoulder and pushed me down, rewarding me for my loyalty.

I was face-to-face with her bulge. She rubbed it with her manicured fingertips and then she slid her panties down to show me her cock. Her hand took the back of my head and pulled me in so that I could suck her off. I will admit that it was a nice reward. I bobbed my head back and forth, sucking her smooth shaft. I could feel it throbbing and growing. I gripped it with my hand and pulled her foreskin back so I could see that beautiful, feminine tip. I gave it a lick and she moaned.

Maybe this was all she needed to help her relax.

I tightened my grip and started to pump her. I tickled her tip with the tip of my tongue. She gasped and grabbed on tight to the nearby door handle. "John!" she whispered. "You're going to make me cum!"

"Isn't that the idea?" I asked, and then I bent

forward and sucked her hard and fast, slobbering all over her beautiful shaft. She was rock-hard now, veins thick and pumping. I gagged when she pushed into the back of my throat, but I managed to keep going.

"Oh God," she moaned. "Don't stop! Don't stop, John! Don't stop!"

With the thumb of my free hand, I reached around her. I found her tight hole and began to tease it, rubbing in circles until it felt like time to push into her body. She groaned. "Shit," she mumbled. "Just like that. Oh God, just like that, John. Oh my fucking God, that feels so good. Yes! Don't stop sucking my hard cock. Oh God, John! You're going to make me cum in your fucking mouth! Oh God! Oh God!" She was getting louder and louder, tensing up harder. Her legs were shaking. A high-pitched sound was now coming out of her mouth as she tried to hold back her orgasm.

"Fuck! I'm coming! I'm coming!"

I pumped her hard and opened wide, letting her blast onto my tongue.

It took a minute to clean up. I thought we were only gone for a few minutes, but apparently we'd been gone for close to an hour. Now, our teammates were looking for us. Bruce pulled me aside. "Where were you?" he asked, red with nervousness.

"I was giving her a pep talk," I said, blushing.

"We're on in five minutes," he said. "Are you guys ready or not?"

I smiled and nodded my head.

Our lateness was probably for the best. Billie Rae didn't have time to be nervous. We were swept away to get ready, put into our seats. The tournament had been running behind, and now they were scrambling to make up time. They cut out the five minutes of press photos, telling the photographers they had to take their photos while we played, not before. We were thrust right into character selection. I could still taste cum when the game began.

I was a bit dazed, heart still racing from our little naughty act in the back hallway. I wasn't as sharp as I probably should have been—and I didn't even notice that Billie Rae had successfully killed the enemy mid-lane player and taken out their tower, all within the first seven minutes of the game.

The enemy tried to stage an ambush on her—certainly something they'd planned before the game even started, after seeing her low stats... but their attempt failed; Billie Rae was ready for them, with a snare trap set within range of the tower. Two enemies died trying to kill her, and she hardly even took a hit. She was outsmarting them, using the stats from her bad start as bait. By the twenty-minute mark, Billie Rae was ruthlessly overpowered, storming up that middle lane like an invincible force.

The opposing team made the foolish mistake of repeating their strategy in the next game, thinking we wouldn't see it coming twice in a row. But Billie

Rae was ready for them—and Bruce instantly recognized the pattern and acted accordingly, planning his own pushes with their failed ambushes. That second game was even faster than the first.

Now, we were 2-2, with one round-robin match left.

But now, we had momentum. Billie Rae was smiling, back into her element. Her name was now near the middle of that long list.

We were steamrolling through games now. It was 8:00 PM when we went into that final match. It was against a hard team… at least they should have been hard to beat. But they hardly put up a fight. We were firing on all cylinders: pushing the top lane aggressively, successfully ambushing in the jungle, and Race-Star was racking up kills without getting killed even once. We won both matches, not needing a third.

And just like that, we were into the quarter finals. We wouldn't be going home early after all.

But the tournament wasn't over yet. There were still two more days of tough games if we were going to get an invite to Nationals.

CHAPTER 13

*O*ur quarter-final match was on the morning of that Saturday, in that convention centre in Montreal, Quebec. We were playing against FFG, Force-Five Gaming, again. We beat them the day before, but it felt a bit like a lucky win. We knew they weren't going to go so easy on us this time. When we faced them the day before, they came into the match 2-0. They only needed to win one of their next three matches. Now, they were fighting off elimination.

And… it didn't help that we were all feeling a bit unwell from the previous night. The excitement of our comeback turned into a few drinks into the hotel bar, and a few drinks turned into a few too many drinks. Race-Star ended up in the bathroom, throwing up all night. Gobbler met some chick at the bar; she was sixty-four-years-old with a blonde wig and stiff lip injections; they went away together and it took us all morning to find him—and to wake him up.

Erin had met a guy at the bar and gone back to his hotel with him; we still had no idea where she was; luckily, she was an alternate.

And then there was the very, very awkward wakeup call that I got... with Billie Rae. Our alarm didn't succeed in waking either of us up. We were sharing a bed, with her in my arms, her naked body against mine. Bruce tried knocking at the door, apparently, but had no success; but the room was booked in his name, so he was able to get a key card from the front desk so he could let himself in. That's when he saw us together.

We woke up to him roaring. "We're late!"

We both turned white when we saw him. "It—It's not what it looks like," I said, jumping out of the bed, forgetting that I was ass-naked. It didn't help that I pulled the blanket off as I jumped out of bed, revealing the fact that Billie Rae was also naked.

It also didn't help that there was that sex smell in the air. We all know that smell—it's a bit sweet, a but musty… it's not necessarily unpleasant, but it's undeniable. "We'll talk about this later," Bruce growled, and then he stormed out of the room.

I knew we were in trouble. I knew that talk was going to be more than just, 'Don't do it again.' There was a good chance it would mean me getting booted from the team. Billie Rae was probably safe thanks to her contract that she'd made specifically with Centennial Greens, our primary sponsor. I didn't have any special protections. I didn't have a stream that brought in thousands of fans. I didn't have a special connection to Horatio. Horatio only really cared about two people on that team: Bruce and Billie Rae. And there was a good chance that he would have preferred Tuesday playing jungle, since her beautiful blonde hair and big round boobs would bring in more fans than I was bringing in as a man in his mid-thirties.

"Head in the game, guys," Bruce growled into his mic after we lost that first round. It was a best-of-five. We still had a lot of losing left before we were out. "Where's the focus? Race-Star, I want you to push harder at the start. And BR-Cat—you need to land those creep kills. Look how many denies they got on mid."

"I'm sorry," Billie Rae said. She stretched out her arms, putting on her best focussed face.

But I was still thinking about being kicked off the team for fornicating with a teammate. I was dreading the awkward meeting.

I tried hard not to think about that; we had games to win.

That next game was off to a rough start. They tricked us all, ambushing me in our jungle, killing me handily before anyone could react. It was an early disadvantage that we spent the whole game working against. But we chipped our way back into the fight, getting a pick here, a tower there... Soon, it was an even game. Bruce, who was the second-highest ranked player in the whole tournament, gave us a lead after an impressive splash attack that killed three of their players at once, caught completely off-guard as they tried to escape a mid-push.

Now, Bruce was overpowered, and he was the last person the other team wanted to have an advantage. He knew how to use it… and he used it to win the game a few minutes later, pushing hard on the bottom lane while we cleaned out their top lane, mid lane, and jungle.

The series was tied 1-1. We were sent on a fifteen-minute break so they could run ads. During that break, Gobbler came up to me. "I heard you fucked Billie Rae last night," he said with a grin, glaring into my eyes. "You cheeky fuck." He punched me on the shoulder; it was supposed to be playful, but it hurt like hell.

"I don't want to talk about it," I blushed.

"Why not? You should be proud, brother. She's hot. I was going to try fucking her… but I was going to wait until the end of the season first." He was laughing, as if it was funny.

"It wasn't what it looked like," I said. "I just… I want to keep things professional."

"Is that your way of saying it was a drunken

mistake or something, J-Rock?" He chuckled. And I saw it as an opportunity. Maybe if I could convince Bruce that it was just a drunken accident, that it wasn't a romance... after all, the contract that we all signed said 'no relationships'; a drunken fling isn't a relationship. "We were both drunk," I said. "It meant nothing."

He grinned. "So if I were to go for her at the end of the season, you wouldn't be pissed?"

I laughed, trying to swallow my feelings. "I couldn't care less," I said.

"Between you and me," he whispered. "Even if we win here, I don't think her season is going to go on for much longer. That Horatio guy is doing an open-tryout for new players—to replace Griswold Gamer... Well, I can't help but think he's just going to rebuild mid completely."

He gave me another 'playful' punch. "So I may get a shot at her sooner rather than later."

I guess he really didn't know about her special contract.

"Let's just focus on winning this next game."

We did not win the next game. The other team came out swinging, determined to get the momentum moving in their favour. They hit us hard with coordinated attacks. Their moves were planned and practised. We made the mistake of letting them pick their favourite champions instead of trying to force them into picking less-practised champions. They bruised us up, making us very nervous going into game-four.

It was possibly our last game. Bruce gathered us around for a pep talk. He glared at me with that dark look, as if he was blaming the loss on my little fling with Billie Rae. The loss wasn't anyone's fault; we were just outplayed. "We can do this," I said, turning to look away from that intimidating glare.

I had to play my best game ever. I had to play a perfect game. I couldn't make a single mistake.

So I went into the game focussed. I bit hard on my tongue and dialled myself in.

Bruce made a rare slip-up at the beginning of the game, letting his guard down, allowing the enemy team to strike him down… and then it happened to Race-Star as well. Gobbler scrambled to go from lane to lane, trying to be present at every ambush— but the enemy just always seemed to know where we were, as if they used their early earnings on wards.

At the fifteen-minute mark, it seemed like we were doomed… and then I heard Billie Rae's voice in my ear as she spoke into her little mic. "Come with me, John," she said softly. I looked at the map and saw that she was on the edge of enemy territory, hidden in a shadowed nook where she wouldn't be seen.

It seemed insane; she wanted to go into enemy territory while we were losing: a suicide mission... but we needed to take a gamble if we were going to claw our way back in.

But I'd forgotten one thing: Billie Rae was smart; she had a wicked game sense that I could only dream of having. She figured one thing out very fast: if they had wards in our jungle, then they probably didn't have any wards in their own. And why would they? When you're winning and pushing towards the enemy base, you don't need to think about your own end, because nobody is stupid enough to go that deep when playing from behind.

Billie Rae knew the enemy champions well enough to know what buffs they would try to get before pushing, which meant they needed to kill certain creeps in their jungle before moving into our end to push. Look—I've said it a million times—you don't need to understand the game details. Long story short, Billie Rae knew that their mid-lane player would be in that specific spot at that specific time, alone. She knew we could kill him together— and she was right.

But we didn't just retreat after killing the enemy, like the enemy would assume we would do. Instead, we darted left to take out an enemy tower. The enemy must have thought we were insane, playing suicidal tactics... Maybe they thought we were trying to create a distraction, because that's how they reacted; they backed up and prepared for a push that wasn't coming.

We weren't in the lead after taking out that tower, but we did have them scrambling, confused, on their toes. And that state of confusion was perfect for Bruce, who had ungodly game sense. He jumped on every opportunity: every little slip. Now, the enemy had their eyes on their mini-maps, watching for sneak attacks from Billie Rae and me. They weren't watching for Bruce, who was suddenly playing a flawless game. He killed one, two, three enemies. Race-Star made a strong recovery while the enemy was regrouping to push Bruce back; Race-Star snuck in and took out a tower, and then another—and he was gone before the enemy appeared to take him out. Now, Bruce was at the other end of the map, pushing up the lane again, forcing the enemy to trek across the whole playfield one more time.

We ended up winning the game; the enemy never

got that momentum back. And for the rest of the series, the enemy team remained on edge, scared to take risks, scared that Billie Rae was going to make some crazy suicide attack in areas they assumed that they were safe.

We advanced to the semi-final. An intense relief washed over us. Finally, we didn't have to play in desperation mode. A third-place finish was still a ticket to Nationals, meaning we could lose our semi and still qualify for Nationals if we won our final.

But I'll just skip ahead and tell you that we won our semi-final, winning that ticket to Nationals—and, not to brag, but I was the MVP in two out of four games. Billie-Rae was the MVP in our other win. Our enemy only won a single game—and it was a narrow victory.

Billie Rae and I worked like a single entity. We played that game as if we could communicate telepathically. I suppose I'd played with her enough to simply know when she wanted to strike, when she wanted to ambush, and when she needed to back off. And Bruce knew that we were the reason for that series win; he went straight to us after the game to hug us. It was a bit weird, feeling his thick arms wrapping around me, squeezing me tight. I never pegged him as a hugger… and I didn't realize he was that strong; though I shouldn't have been so shocked, seeing as he kept dumbbells next to his computer at the house, which he pumped between practise rounds. "I could kiss you on the lips!" he said to me.

"Please don't."

The relief was beyond intense. Not only did we stamp our ticket to Nationals, but I felt like I was off the hook for being caught naked in bed with a teammate. And to make it even better, Billie Rae was now smiling, finished with her slump. To be honest, I couldn't help but feel like I helped her to get that stress out by fooling around with her—not that I was taking credit for her success... Okay, maybe I was taking a bit of credit.

We were all beaming and smiling as we went to sit for a couple of hours in the stands. Fans saw us and screamed like teen girls (many were teen girls). They wanted pictures with us. They wanted signatures. One girl handed me a drawing she'd made of me, with my headset on. She told me she'd spent sixteen hours on it. I was flustered, blushing all over.

With all the attention we were getting, I almost didn't notice HGA stomping Pluto Gaming Corp into the ground, winning three straight to advance to that A-Final round. And guess who was the MVP in all three games? That's right: Franklin Griswold, aka Griswold Gaming.

The rest of our team didn't even notice HGA had won their semi; they were too busy celebrating our own victory, and I felt a bit like I took that happiness away from them when I said, "Hey guys. I think we're up soon. We should figure out what our strategy is to face HGA." I watched as their faces turned pale. They all looked towards the main stage, which was now emptying out. Billie Rae looked especially nervous, knowing she was going to be facing the tournament MVP in her middle lane.

CHAPTER 14

It did matter who won. Sure, both teams were guaranteed spots at Nationals in Vancouver, British Columbia, but the winner got to skip the round-robin round at Nationals: five best-of-three matches. The winner of that particular qualifier got to join the winners of the other three qualifiers in the quarter finals, which would leave eight teams battling for the remaining four spots. Now, as you can imagine, that is an enormous advantage to go into a tournament with.

Also, the winner of that final got their expenses paid by the tournament. Now, for us, that didn't really matter, but Horatio, with Centennial Greens, would have been thrilled to find out he was getting reimbursed for all of those plane tickets. It certainly would have motivated him to continue funding that team for another year.

So, even though our ticket to Vancouver in one week had already been stamped, there was still intense pressure to win.

I won't bog you down with the game details. I'll just say this: we played well... but it wasn't enough. Game after game, it seemed like we were playing just fine, and then we would suddenly find ourselves scrambling. Horizon Gaming was a strong team, loaded with powerhouse players. There was always some MVP-level player there to pounce on the smallest mistakes. In the first game, Race-Star attempted to ambush the enemy jungler and was instantly caught in a snare. Killing Race-Star was enough of a boost to give them an unstoppable momentum.

The next game, the enemy team targeted Gobbler aggressively. It was a tactic that we just weren't expecting, and we weren't prepared for it. They stopped him from gaining experience. They stopped him from earning money. By the twenty-minute mark, it really started to sting, not having a support that could heal us or buff us or give us visibility of that playing field. It was enough of a disadvantage that we just couldn't keep up.

And the third game, facing elimination, Franklin decided to prove that he was the better player, that he deserved that main spot on our team. He went at Billie Rae with relentless intensity. I tried to be there each time, but he was playing a flawless game. Even with the two of us together, we couldn't seem to control him. He was a force of nature, determined to prove that Bruce had made a huge mistake. And in that game, he made his point. By the twenty-minute mark, he was overpowered. He had more kills than anyone in the game, and more money, and more gear. He could take on three men at once without losing even half of his health. He ruined us…

We lost 0-3. For about twenty minutes, our spirits were crushed. We were all quiet. It felt like an anti-climactic end to a hard-fought weekend. We rose up from starting with two straight losses in the round-robin, and then we were so close to winning the tournament… Now, we were watching as Franklin held up his gold medal, presented by the Canadian E-Sports Commissioner. There was no silver medal to be handed out…

But then the commissioner came to us and handed us tickets to the tournament in Vancouver. They weren't real tickets: just novelties to let us know that we qualified. It was a nice reminder that we achieved what we went there to achieve. We were able to smile again. We were all relieved. Sadly, we wouldn't get to skip the round-robin in Vancouver, but we did get to compete in Vancouver.

We still had a chance at redemption, in one week's time...

That gave us one week to practise... and to celebrate our team's first real achievement.

Bruce surprised us all that Monday morning, after we landed back at the Calgary International Airport, when he said, "We'll resume practise tomorrow. You guys can enjoy the rest of the day off."

I thought that we was going to approach me when we got to the house in Red Deer, to talk about the incident with Billie Rae, but he didn't say anything; he just gave me a look: a long look that made my heart flutter. It was like he was saying, 'I'll keep my mouth shut about this as long as you promise not to let it become an issue.' Or maybe he was saying, 'Just don't do it again.'

Well, we did it again. It was our way of celebrating... It didn't help that Horatio had ten bottles of champagne sent to the house—and a private chef showed up to cook everyone in the house a steak dinner. Oh, but that wasn't all. Horatio was full of multi-millionaire surprises.

He was a rich man who was passionate about E-sports. He'd dreamed about owning an E-sports franchise like this one. Bruce told me that night after consuming a few drinks: "This is his third team. He tried to make teams in Quebec and Toronto, but they didn't make it beyond Qualifiers, so he let them dissolve." It was shocking news to hear: Bruce was essentially telling me that our team would have ceased to exist if we hadn't qualified for Nationals—and he knew it. The pressure on him must have been enormous, carrying that little nugget of knowledge...

There was a knock at the door around 8:00 PM, after we'd finished eating our chef-cooked steaks. A man in a suit was standing there, hands clasped at his waist. "The limo is ready when you're ready to go," the man said with his chin up. It was another Horatio surprise: a limo ride to the city's busiest bar, where the VIP lounge was reserved. Now, this was Red Deer—not some big metropolis, so it wasn't exactly a Manhattan VIP experience, but the drinks were all paid for, desserts came to us, delivered by a local bakery that had been paid extra to make that special delivery.

A photographer showed up, hired to take promotional photos from flattering angles. And finally, the night ended with Horatio showing up (around midnight) to give us all gifts: Rolex watches for the men and diamond necklaces for the women. All in all, I think Horatio spent a quarter million dollars pampering us that night. I was beginning to think he was closer to being a billionaire than we all realized.

Waiting for us back at the house were gift baskets, one in each room. Each basket was filled with personal gifts: expensive liquor bottles, soaps, gift certificates for restaurants and shops—and a note that said, 'Keep winning.'

I wasn't used to being spoiled like this.

I went to show Billie Rae what I received in my basket, and that's when I saw her wearing a tiny, sparkly dress. I froze at the sight of her. That dress made her glow and shine. She looked at me, blushing. "It was in my basket," she said. She was wearing sparkly heels on her feet, red on the bottom. She just looked like she was wearing ten thousand dollars on her body—more if you counted the diamond necklace around her neck.

"Sheesh," I said, eyeing her body.

And I knew that Bruce had silently asked me not to do it again… but how could I resist? I couldn't resist a sight like that. I had to have her. I had to push her down onto the bed. I had to squeeze her perky breasts. I had to grind myself against her throbbing erection. We closed her bedroom door and we went at it.

I fucked her until her ass was filled with cream, and then I let her push her erection into my body. I bounced on her lap for fifteen minutes. I bounced hard, until my cock was hard again—and then I kept bouncing until my cock was erupting again, untouched, spewing cum left and right, coating her naked breasts. One shot landed right on her erect nipple. She took my head and pulled me down, making me suck that nipple, making me taste my own ejaculation.

I badly wanted to sleep with her, in her bed, with her in my arms... but we were able to fight that temptation... after cuddling together warmly for two hours. I was able to pull myself away around 4:30 AM. I was able to return to my room where I got a few hours of sleep, feeling cold without her, but still somehow feeling like our hearts were together. When we saw each other in the morning, we were both giggly. We were both blushing, unable to stay away from each other. She snuck a kiss on me when nobody was looking. I snuck one on her when nobody was looking. During on game, she reached down and held my hand while we were waiting for our teammates to select their champions.

Those high spirits rubbed off on our game. We were playing great League of Legends. Billie Rae was once again a powerful force, often earning that MVP title. That Tuesday was great.

Then, Wednesday came—and Tuesday had a surprise... She came into the room around midday and announced that she had to leave the team. She was pale in the face, looking perturbed. "I didn't want it to end this way, but some matters came to my attention..."

"What matters?" Bruce asked.

Tuesday asked to speak with Bruce in private, and then they went upstairs, leaving the rest of us to break for lunch. They were upstairs for a long time, and nobody knew what was happening. Now, we were down to six players on our team, which was the absolute minimum required to be considered a complete team (every team needed at least one alternate player, most had three to five).

Gobbler suggested she realized that she was never going to get a spot on the main roster, so her presence there was pointless. Maybe she'd discovered some recording of Bruce talking about it with Horatio… but my gut was telling me that something worse was behind this. Tuesday's face just suggested something much more… sinister. When she came downstairs, she looked into my eyes. She paused for a moment, batting those beautiful eyelashes. She smiled sorrowfully and then she turned her gaze to the floor. "Goodbye, everyone," she said. She took a minute going from player to player, hugging, crying… every player except for Billie Rae.

I tried not to think too much into it. We really needed to focus on training for the upcoming Nationals event… There were four Qualifiers each year, but there was only one Nationals, and there was only one winner at Nationals, winning that ticket to the World Circuit where the big money was waiting to be won. If we were going to have a shot at real fame and fortune, we had to win this tournament in Vancouver. We would have to beat Franklin and Horizon Gaming, as well as the other three teams that won their qualifiers—not to mention all of the teams, like ours, who made it into the round-robin event...

I had to focus hard. I had to concentrate. I couldn't even let Billie Rae get into my head, which was hard to do, especially that evening when she did her weekly steaming-in-lingerie session. Now, I knew who she was and I could find her stream. I'd seen the replays of her in those tight, skimpy outfits. My God, she looked stunning. Tens of thousands of men tuned in to jerk off to the sight of her. No, it wasn't pornographic. She wasn't inserting toys into herself or flashing her breasts. She was just an E-Girl, being a little extra naughty to increase her viewership. I couldn't blame her; she was a hustler. She was making a name for herself, and that fame was part of the reason she made it onto our team. And because of her, our team had the second biggest fanbase in the country, after just a month of existing. We had some of the biggest sponsorships. We received thousands of fan messages each day, largely thanks to Billie Rae's beauty, and her willingness to sit in front of a live camera, dressed like a Playboy bunny. She was doing it now, upstairs, speaking sensually to her fans while she played on an alternate account, where it didn't matter so much if she won or lost. I wanted to watch that stream…

No—I had to focus. I had to keep practising my build orders, my grinding speed. I still needed to perfect my denies; it wasn't something I practised much as a jungler, but Bruce wanted me to swing to the middle lane whenever Billie Rae had to retreat, to deny the enemy the extra money…

But the sound of Billie Rae's occasional giggling upstairs made it hard to focus… And then the text message from Tuesday made it even harder to focus.

"We need to talk. Can you meet me at the cafe down the street?"

"When?" I wrote back.

"As soon as you're free. I'm there now."

My heart was sent aflutter. I had no idea what was happening. And to make it stranger, she added, "Don't tell anyone that you're meeting me."

I told Bruce that I had an important family phone call to make. We were just two days away from flying to Vancouver, and we were trying not to waste a single moment of potential training, so every excuse to step away had to be valid. And believe me when I say that coming up with a valid excuse to step away wasn't so easy. Even if someone stood up to use the bathroom, Bruce would perk up and say, "Where are you going?" Sometimes he would even tell them to hold it until a better moment came up. No second could be wasted—but I knew that Tuesday had something important to tell me.

She was there, sitting in the back corner of the cafe, dressed unlike her usual self. Now, she was wearing a hoodie, black, with some anime girl face on the front of it. Her long black sleeves covered her hands, except for her fingernails, and her hood was on her blonde hair. She wasn't wearing makeup; I don't know that I'd ever seen her without makeup before, and now, I was shocked to see that she was even prettier without it. She had that natural beauty that every woman in the world wishes they had, with freckles I had no idea that she had. She motioned for me to sit, and then she smiled. "I got you a coffee. I know you guys are staying up late tonight to practise, so I made it extra strong."

"Thanks," I said. I looked into her eyes and saw that same sorrowful smile that she left the house with earlier. "I don't get why you left the team. I'm pretty sure that Bruce was going to put you into a few games in the round-robin in Vancouver. I think you're a better player than me."

She giggled. "Oh, please," she said. "Don't be silly, John."

"Regardless. I still think you should have stayed on the team. If not at the tournament, he would have played you in exhibition matches."

"I know he would have," she smiled. "That's not why I left the team though, John."

She kept staring into my eyes. I have to admit that I was feeling rather intimidated. It took me some getting used to being around Billie Rae, who was, physically-speaking, far out of my league. But Tuesday was in a whole different league—no offence to Billie Rae. Billie Rae was definitely the ideal E-Girl: every game boy's dream chick... but Tuesday was the kind of girl who could have been on the cover of Playboy. She could have been an international supermodel. She could have made millions of dollars by simply posting photos of her face on Instagram, and sponsors would have thrown money at her. She didn't need a gamer niche. She didn't have to sit in lingerie to get male attention.

Yes, I can admit fully and honestly that Tuesday was, traditionally, more attractive than Billie Rae.

Nine out of ten men would probably agree—but that's not me saying that Billie Rae was any less adorable and stunning than she was.

She was quiet now, blushing, smiling. "Okay, I guess I should just come out with it," she said. "I left for two reasons… One, if I were to stay, I would be breaching my contract, and I don't believe in breaking promises. And two, I learned some things that just didn't sit well with me… about certain players on the team. And… well, I think you should know what I learned so you can know what you're being associated with. This information came to me from Franklin. He emailed me this morning, and I took some time to verify it—and it's true."

I could only assume that she was talking about the secret contract between Horatio and Billie Rae, but I tried my best to play dumb. I wasn't supposed to know anything about it.

"You're being very vague," I said. "And you have me worried."

She looked down at her coffee and swirled it in her mug. Her mug was nearly empty, as if she'd been there for a long time already, waiting for me. Maybe it took her a long time to build up the courage to invite me to that cafe. "I won't lie, John. You should be a bit worried. It's not something that I want to be associated with. It's nothing illegal, but it's not what I would call… moral."

"What is it?" I asked, wriggling in my seat with anticipation. I felt cold all over, knowing there was a good chance that she was about to crush my dream. It really had seemed like things were too good to be true up until that point…

"Okay, where do I start…" she said, looking up and taking a deep breath. "So, Bruce was going to keep you on the roster for Nationals," she continued. "But for Worlds, he was going to put me in, and you were going to become the alternate. I was told that a long time ago, before I even joined the team."

I paused for a moment. "Wait… Why?"

"Horatio has sponsorships lined up. He has investors with interests, and part of fulfilling those interests is having certain names attached to the team. BR-Cat is one of those names. She brings in a huge viewership… Franklin somehow found a copy of her contract and sent it to me. Franklin was never going to be on the team."

I bit my tongue, pretending to be surprised.

"They're only keeping you on the team because they think there's a better shot at making the World Circuit with you in the jungle. Horatio doesn't care about winning tournaments at Worlds. As long as the team is registered, the sponsorships will go ahead. Part of my agreement was being the poster girl for the team. They were going to put me on posters, swag—all of that."

"Well," I said. "I suppose I can't blame them. You're beautiful, and you're a well-known name in the business." My heart felt cold. I felt sick, knowing that I was going to be thrown aside… but being an alternate on a major team was still better than working at Game Stop, even if it meant never playing another game after Nationals… Alternates still share the winnings if there are any… though it wasn't sounding like there would be any… But I would still be pampered with the rest of the team. I would still get a paycheque like the other players...

But did I really want to be a bench warmer?

She blushed. "You're sweet, John," she said. "I really like you. That's why I felt like I had to tell you all of this. When I signed the contract and made the agreement, I never really thought much about who would be the alternate... now I just feel awful about the whole thing. It's not at all what I wanted, and you deserve to play. I had my glory days. I'm old now."

"Are you even thirty?" I asked with a small laugh.

"I'm thirty-six, as a matter of fact!" she said, taking me by surprise.

She looked into my eyes again, making my heart flutter once more.

"So is that it?" I asked. "That's what you wanted to tell me?" Sure, it was a shock and it wasn't sitting well with me, but it wasn't nearly as bad as I was expecting. I thought that she was going to tell me that Horatio had been using the team to embezzle money or something.

"Sort of," she said. "Nobody on the team but Bruce knows... Oh, and Billie Rae knows."

"What does she know?" I asked.

"She knew that she would get the main spot

instead of Franklin, and she knew that I was going to replace you after Nationals," she said.

"How do you know that she knew that last part?" I asked. My heart skipped a beat.

Tuesday laughed. "Well, she was there when we signed the contract with Horatio."

My heart plunged into the pit of my stomach. Billie Rae knew that I was going to be tossed aside, and she never said anything?

Now, I was speechless. I opened my mouth to speak, but I couldn't muster up any words. I felt betrayed. I felt sick to my stomach.

"I'm sorry, John," she said. "I know this is all a big dream for you, playing on this team. But these teams always have their share of drama. Franklin told me that he's going to make the news public before Vancouver. I feel so bad for Franklin... He really never had a chance. Everyone thinks he overreacted, but can you imagine being in his position? He sold his condo to move out here. He gave up everything. And they were just using him... Well, I guess you might have an idea now of how that feels, though with me gone, I'm sure they will keep you on the roster... unless they can find another poster boy or girl to replace you. If I were you, I would be on high alert. If Centennial signs some high-calibre player—

even someone past their prime like me—just be on high alert. Okay?"

"O—Okay," I said.

"And do me a favour," she said. "Stay away from that Billie Rae girl."

"She really means well," I said, feeling like I had to defend her, despite what I was being told.

"She comes off that way," Tuesday said, biting her bottom lip. "But Franklin found some dirt on her, and it's not pretty."

I hesitated for a moment. "W—What dirt?"

"Lots of dirt," she said. "And it's all coming out before the tournament. It's all stuff you're going to be hearing at the press conference tomorrow night."

"Like what?" I asked, feeling my skin turning pale.

"Well, for one, Billie Rae isn't even her real name. She was born male."

"She's trans… so what?" I said.

"I know she's trans, John. I'm not talking about her being trans. Let's just say that Billie Rae isn't her first name as a girl. She had to change it after she was caught scamming guys into buying her Amazon gift cards a couple of years ago."

"What?" I said.

She nodded her head. "Back then, she was Taylor

Rae. She was ranked in the top 2000 on League and then, when everyone found out that she was scamming guys by pretending to be into them... you know, romantically—she deactivated her account. She closed her social profiles. She even dyed her hair."

"This all sounds crazy," I said, shaking my head.

"But it's true!" Tuesday gasped. "And Franklin proved it. Look." She took out her phone and showed me the evidence that was sent to her: screenshots from old social media accounts, with Billie Rae's old pictures: her with black hair... but it was definitely her. I knew those glittering eyes. I knew that soft, petite body. But that name: Taylor Rae... she'd never mentioned it before. Then, Tuesday showed me the archived player profile of Taylor Rae, and screenshots taken by the man who claimed to have been scammed by her. In the screenshot, she was offering pictures of her body in exchange for an Amazon gift card. "She was doing it to a bunch of guys," Tuesday said. "And she was probably selling the gift cards for cash. It's a classic scam that's almost impossible to trace. Now, she accepts gift cards as gifts on her stream. She's probably selling them all. I guess there's nothing illegal with what she's doing... but I'm sure we can both agree that it's not so moral."

It was all so hard to believe.

"And that's not even everything," said Tuesday, eyes wide now. "When she was still a dude, she—I mean, *he* was caught cheating in a Starcraft tournament." She pulled up the images on her phone. "He was kicked out of the tournament after they discovered a sex toy on him."

"What?" I said.

"It was in the news and everything. He had a remote-controlled vibrator between his legs—maybe even up his ass. He had a friend sitting in the stands, watching the match on the screen. Whenever his opponent would prepare an attack, the friend would buzz the vibrator. Basically what happened is, someone in the stands saw the guy with the remote and got suspicious. Some famous chess player was caught doing the same thing a year earlier." She showed me the article, and that's when my heart truly stopped beating for a moment.

"He had to drop off the Starcraft circuit. Apparently he got a job at a Game Stop and just dropped off the face of the earth."

"Rick..." I said, reading that name. And there was his picture: Rick, my old boss at Game Stop. I admired Rick so much... but now, I couldn't believe what I was seeing. I couldn't believe what Tuesday was telling me... but the proof was right in front of me—and it was all about to come out.

"Uh, thanks for bringing this all to my attention," I said. I nearly fell over as I stood up. My legs were trembling. My heart was racing. This new information wasn't sitting well with me, churning in my gut, filling my veins with icy coldness.

I'd been having sex with my old boss. Billie Rae knew who I was this whole time, but chose not to tell me. And worse, she knew that I was going to be booted out from my spot if we won Nationals.

If I was to believe what Tuesday was telling, then Billie Rae had essentially been conspiring against me, and gladly accepting sexual intimacy in return.

"John, wait," Tuesday said as I took a few steps away from that small cafe table.

"Bruce is going to wonder where I went," I said, head still spinning.

"There's something else I have to tell you," she said.

"W—What is it?" I said. I wasn't sure that I could handle anything else. I was already starting to think about my job at Game Stop again... which wasn't even there waiting for me. I left on bad terms—not like Billie Rae, who had been travelling back and forth to finish out her two week's notice, knowing that there was a very good chance the team would be dissolved and she would need to seek out a job again. If she had really cared about me, she would have advised me to do the same thing...

"John..." Tuesday went on. She turned her gaze to the table and blushed hard all over. "I really like you. And, uh, I know girls don't generally ask boys out on dates... but maybe we could go out for coffee together, in Quebec City."

"Quebec City?" I asked.

"I was talking to my old team captain, and he's starting a new team for next season. It will be based out of Quebec City, and he's starting it with his girl-friend. She plays support and he's an ADC. Long story short, because of their relationship, they won't have any weird no-relationship rules in their contract. I told him about you, and he likes the idea of having you in as the jungler."

"W—What about you?" I asked.

She smiled. "Well, I've been playing so much on mid, with Billie Rae always doing her streams and whatnot... I'm actually getting pretty good. I thought I would spend the rest of the year practising mid. This whole thing is just an idea right now, John.

But… I really like you. You're sweet. I'd love to grab a proper coffee with you sometime… when I'm not just giving you bad news."

"I, uh… I'll let you know," I said. "I just really need to figure out what I'm doing here."

She smiled. "I'll email you my number. I'm leaving for Quebec on Monday—so I'll be gone before you're back from Vancouver. But… if things don't work out with Centennial, come to Quebec. I can get you a streaming gig that will run the rest of the season—just for some living money, or whatever. Then, maybe we can move into a new team house. It's all just… stuff to think about."

"Thanks, Tuesday," I smiled. I looked to the floor, and then I left the cafe.

CHAPTER 15

I didn't bring up what I knew. I spent that night doing some of my own digging, trying to verify what Tuesday had told me. I found the article she showed me, and there was a picture of Rick, formerly known as T2-StarCraft, back when he played StarCraft. He was a highly ranked player, just sixteen-years-old. He went to many tournaments. I managed to find dozens of videos of him playing… and they all had the comments in the comment sections: 'Isn't this the guy who shoved a dildo in his ass to cheat?' 'Whatever happened to this tool?' 'If you turn your volume up loud enough, you can hear the buzzing!'

I didn't get much sleep. Billie Rae was there in the kitchen the next morning, though I wasn't sure that I could even call her Billie Rae anymore. Was that even her name, legally? My heart was still aflutter—and it got worse when she approached me, smiling. When nobody was looking, she grabbed my hand and smiled, saying, "Good morning, Johnny."

"Hey," I said. Her hand felt strangely cold. Had she been using me this whole time? Was she just trying to use me to get the team to that pro level? Why had she kept this a secret from me?

"Everything okay?" she asked.

"I don't know," I said. "I guess... I just feel a bit weird."

"Nervous?" she said. "Are you all packed for the flight?"

"Not yet," I said. "I should probably go and do that." I stared into her eyes. Now, I could see Rick behind those eyes. I recognized her now, and I couldn't figure out how I didn't see it before; it seemed so obvious! It should have been even more obvious when I found out that she was trans. My God, there were so many clues, and I ignored all of them.

And now, she was smiling, assuming that I was still totally oblivious.

"Bruce said we can take the morning off," she

said. "I thought that maybe we could sneak away and get a coffee at that cafe down the road."

"I don't think that's a great idea," I said.

"Why not?"

I stared into her eyes. "I still have to pack."

She giggled. "You're a guy. How long could that take?"

I bit down on the side of my tongue. I wanted so badly to call her out—I even thought of doing it a moment later when the others entered the room. I wanted to call her out in front of everyone; they all deserved to know the truth before it came out to humiliate everyone. That news was going to come out before that press conference. It wasn't fair that Gobbler and Race-Star and Kitten Krusader were all going to be caught off-guard by it; at least I had some warning.

And I had to think hard about what I was going to do: should I go on this trip? If I dropped out, the team couldn't compete; we were already at the minimum number of players. Every team needed an alternate. I couldn't let the rest of the team down…

My head was swirling. This position seemed so unfair. Bruce came into the room and eyed me for a moment. I thought about taking him upstairs to discuss my options, but I also didn't want to call out

Tuesday. I didn't want to throw her under the bus, in case there was something in her contract about keeping her lips sealed on this whole controversial matter. But maybe he deserved to be warned too, that all of this information was coming out... unless, of course, he was in on it, with BR-Cat, and with Horatio. Then, he was just as dastardly as the rest of them...

"John?" said Billie Rae, staring into my eyes. "Is something wrong?"

"I don't know," I said. "There's just... someone in my life that's not treating me so nicely."

"What do you mean?" she asked.

"Well, I've been treating them like... royalty. And they'd just been using me. I guess it sucks."

"Do you want to go and talk about it?" she asked, turning a slight shade of white.

"Not really," I said. I stared at her, half-hoping that she would come clean to me. I wanted to think that she had it in her to be an honest girl. I wanted to think that she could be redeemed. I'd made mistakes in my life, and I would hate to think that people were judging me for my past mistakes.

But Billie Rae wasn't coming clean. She was just playing dumb, looking innocent.

Another part of me wanted to warn her. I still

had strong feelings for her, even if she was using me for her own benefit… I didn't want her to end up being humiliated in front of the whole worlds. One-hundred thousand people would be tuning into that press conference: people from all over the world. Billie Rae already knew the sting of public humiliation; did she really deserve to suffer through it again?

I kept my lips sealed. I went up to my room to pack my things. I was going to play in the tournament. I was going to play the games, win or lose. But I made sure to find Bruce before we left for the airport. "What is it?" he asked.

"The press conference tonight," I said.

"What about it?" he asked.

"I won't be attending it."

"What? Why not? You have to. It's in your contract, John." He narrowed his eyes and scowled at me.

"Okay, well, I don't feel like doing it. And there's no alternate, so you don't have many options…"

"What the hell is going on with you!?" Bruce growled. "This isn't like you at all, John."

"If you want me to play this weekend, you'll let me skip the press conference."

"It's not up to you."

"Okay, so boot me from the team then, Bruce," I said, almost grinning as I realized how much power I currently had.

He stared into my eyes. "It almost feels like you're blackmailing me right now, John."

"Is that how it feels?" I asked, biting down on my tongue, not wanting to lash out at him.

Now, we were just glaring at one another. He had a dark gleam in his eyes, suggesting that he was onto me. He knew that I knew something. He knew that I had been let in on the dirt that made Tuesday leave the team. Now, he was struggling to be in control. That standoff lasted a long, long time—and then it ended with silence. He didn't give me permission to skip the conference, but he also didn't push his strictness on me again.

It was a quiet ride to the airport, two hours away. It was a quiet plane ride to Vancouver, and then a quiet trip to the hotel. We were checking into our rooms when Gobbler said, "What the hell is this?" We all looked back to see him looking down at his phone, pale-faced. The news was out. It was only a minute before all of our phones were buzzing: our gamer friends sending us the news, in case we hadn't already seen it.

Bruce looked up at me. His eyes were dark,

cheeks red with humiliation. He now knew that I knew. "I'll see you tomorrow morning for warmup," he said to me. He handed me my room card and then he stormed off towards his own room to prepare for the worst press conference of his life.

Billie Rae was told to skip the press conference, so it was only the four of them on that stage, answering questions while 145,000 people tuned in to watch. "We aren't commenting on that," Bruce said over and over as interviewers asked about Billie Rae's past identity, and about the phoney signing of Franklin Griswold. But the questions just kept coming—and the team was required to spend a full thirty minutes on that stage, answering questions.

Halfway through the conference, there was a knock at my door. I saw Billie Rae through the peephole. She had a hood on her head, hands buried in her hoodie pouch. Her chin was turned down, gaze on the ground. I opened the door with reluctance. "What is it?" I asked.

"Can we talk?"

I didn't want to let her in, but I knew that we needed to find some closure, one way or another. Now, she knew that I knew everything. I had a feeling that I was about to get an apology—but it was too late. Apologies are pointless if they don't come until the wrong doing has already been exposed, as far as I'm concerned.

She closed the door behind her and then stood awkwardly in my quiet room. "I didn't want you to find out like this," she said softly.

"You didn't want me to find out at all," I said.

She looked into my eyes for a brief moment, showing me the redness, showing me that she'd been crying. But I could only assume that she was sad because she'd been caught—not guilty about what she'd done.

"You lied to me," I said.

"I didn't lie," she said. "I just... I was waiting for the right time to tell you certain details."

"As far as I'm concerned, you lied to me."

"I like you," she said, almost as if she was trying to pivot the conversation.

"Bullshit," I said.

"How can you say bullshit!?" she snapped suddenly. "You can't just read one article and think you know everything, John! We made love—many times—did that not mean anything to you?"

"Did it mean anything to you?" I asked. I stared into her eyes and watched her dart her gaze away. "Because it did mean something to me—and that's why it hurt so much when I found out that you've been lying to me."

"For the last time, I never lied!" she said, tearing up. But the tears just didn't seem genuine.

I looked to the floor, realizing this argument was only going to go in circles; there wasn't going to be any resolution. She was going to hold her ground and I was going to hold mine. "I was offered a spot on another team," I said. "I, uh, think I'm going to take it. I'll play this weekend. I'll do my best to get Centennial through to the World Circuit, and then I'm going to tap out. You can easily find a replacement for me once Centennial is in Worlds."

"I don't want to find a replacement; I want you," she said softly. She looked up into my eyes, wiping her cheeks with her sleeves, pushing the tears away. "I guess now is a good time to tell you that you were invited by Horatio because of me. He asked me for player recommendations, and I said you."

"When he asked for recommendations, did you already know that it was just an alternate spot?" I asked.

And there was that guilty look again. "Tuesday's gone now," she said. "The main jungle spot is yours."

"But it was just an alternate spot when you recommended me," I said. "And Horatio never told me that; you never told me that. You were just using me. You were using Franklin. You knew the whole time, and you didn't say anything. Billie—I quit my job for this. I left my house. I could have been applying for colleges… now that will have to wait at least another year. My life went on hold for this— and it was all just a sham!"

"What do you want me to say, John!?" she cried. "I thought it would be a good opportunity for you! Yes, I knew you were going to be Tuesday's alternate. I knew that you wouldn't play in the World Circuit if we qualified, and I knew that if we didn't qualify, the team would dissolve… I knew all of that, and I signed a contract promising that I wouldn't say anything. I wanted to tell you, John! I tried to tell you... but I signed that contract. What do you want from me?"

"All I ever wanted was the truth. And all I got was lies."

She sighed and shook her head. "You're being so dramatic."

"Are you even really a girl?" I asked. "Or is it just a scam?"

She gasped. She stared into my eyes, shocked. "A scam?" she said.

"I know about your past, Billie. I know about Taylor Rae, and I know about the whole StarCraft cheating controversy."

"I never cheated!" she snapped. Then, she began to cry, so she turned away from me. "Oh God, this is so humiliating. This is such a disaster. I just want to go home and crawl into bed and cry."

"I can't understand how you can pretend like you're the victim here. How can you say you never cheated? You were caught."

"I was caught with a vibrator, John! How does that prove anything!?"

I had to roll my eyes. "It was connected to a remote that your friend was controlling." I don't know why I was bothering. I knew she was just going to deny, deny, deny, while acting like a victim.

She wiped her tears away. "It wasn't cheating, John!" she gasped. "It was sexual! That 'friend' was my boyfriend, and we were fooling around! He wasn't using it to warn me when my opponent was attacking; that was just some stupid theory that gained traction."

I stared into her eyes for a long moment, not sure whether or not to believe her.

"It was a stupid theory that ruined my gaming career," she said, wiping her eyes again. "I regret it every day. We were fooling around. Eric, my boyfriend, didn't even know anything about Star-Craft. He had no idea how the game worked; he didn't know nearly enough to 'warn' me about attacks that were coming—and when he was caught with the remote, it wasn't even in the stands like the article said; he was in the bathroom. He was caught… pleasuring himself. And if you don't believe me, you can look up the police report online; he was charged for public indecency. Go ahead and look it up. I'm already this embarrassed, it can't possibly get any worse."

I stood there. I didn't want to look it up. I had no idea whether or not to believe her… but her story sounded plausible. If that police report existed, I suppose it would explain that whole controversy... but that wasn't her only controversy. What about when she was getting men to buy her gift cards?

"I was in the closet back then. I was afraid of coming out as a girl, because I was constantly in the spotlight. After I ran away from that world, I transitioned," she told me. "I started making a new life as a girl. I was finally happy as Taylor. I couldn't play StarCraft anymore, so I started playing League of Legends. I got pretty good. I cracked the top 2000, and then I started gaining some interest from teams. I was playing with this guy, Crash. He was in the top 100 and wanted to start a new team with me. It was good at first. We would play all night long, talking about the team we were going to start, where we would set up our team house, who we would recruit to play with us... but then, he started getting creepy. I told you before, there have been a lot of creeps in my past. Well, Crash got really creepy. He would send me videos of himself... ejaculating all over himself. If I didn't reply instantly, he would start to freak out. He would message me constantly, and he would threaten to cut off contact from me.

"Then, after twenty-four hours of being a spaz, he would flip like a switch. He would apologize profusely, and he would send me gift cards. He'd won a few tournaments before, so he was a millionaire. He would send thousands of dollars worth in gift cards. Things would go back to normal... and then, a few weeks later, he would do it again. He would just get into this strange, aggressive, horny mood, and he would send me all of these pictures and videos. He would demand I send him videos and pictures back, but I just wasn't comfortable with my body then. I was hardly a year into my transition... it was just too much. I told him I couldn't start a team with him, and then he decided to make some shit up about me scamming him."

I didn't know what to think. She seemed to have an excuse for everything.

"Everyone knew Crash. He was like a God in the gaming community, so everyone believed him. He destroyed my reputation, and he threatened to make it so much worse if I leaked any of our conversations. But I can tell you don't believe me... I can show you the messages, the pictures—everything. I have it all.

"I just didn't want the drama, so I stepped away for a year. I created a new alias and played alone. Soon enough, my rank started to rise again. I started playing in those top-ranked games. I played with a lot of the same people that I knew as Taylor. I worked hard to keep my identity a secret. I suppose it was just a matter of time before it all came out.

"But I never did anything illegal. I didn't break any rules. I'm not banned from competing. Controversy just seems to follow me wherever I go. Oh God, I can just tell that you don't believe anything I'm saying. I could easily prove it all in a matter of minutes. I can prove to you that I'm not a liar... but what good would it really do? If you don't believe me now, then there's no point in proving anything. It's obvious that you don't really like me, so I don't really know why I'm bothering to waste my breath right now."

"I do like you," I said. "But regardless of whether or not that's all true..." I really didn't know whether or not to believe her. Tuesday had built her up to be a compulsive liar, and a professional con artist... but that's just not the girl that I knew. "You still brought me onto this team without telling me the reality of my position."

"I thought I was helping you," she sighed. "I thought that it would give you some professional exposure. I thought that some other team would scout you as soon as you played in a few games."

That's exactly what had happened: Tuesday and

her friend had scouted me for their team. And that wouldn't have happened had Billie Rae not recommended me to Horatio. Had Billie Rae not recommended me, I would have still been at Game Stop, dreading every day that I had to work under Chloe, waiting for the day that the store closed down due to irrelevance.

I just didn't know what to believe.

Billie Rae moved to the door. She looked at the ground and sighed. "I, uh, guess I'll see you at warmup tomorrow."

I had a lump the size of a fist in my throat, stopping me from replying to her. I just didn't know what to say.

CHAPTER 16

*VANCOUVER, BRITISH COLUMBIA:
CANADIAN E-SPORTS NATIONAL
COMPETITION*

I walked into the stadium with Gobbler (we shared a room that night). The place was starting to fill up. I did my best to keep my phone off, so that I would see any of the news surrounding our team's controversy. But the controversy news found us. We were spotted by the media. They swarmed us. They wanted to know what we thought about HGA's press conference, and the new updates that had come out concerning Billie Rae, Bruce, and Horatio. Apparently, more information about their secret contracts had been leaked.

I could have stayed to hear more, but I wasn't there to be thrown into the drama, so I slipped away. I just wanted to focus on playing the best game I could. I was starting my gaming career: my dream career. I wasn't going to let the drama of others pull me down.

I tried to get away, but a few interviewers singled me out. "What do you think of the new pictures of your captain, Bruce, meeting with HGA captain, and the deal he tried to make to silence the news about Billie Rae's past?"

I shook my head; it was hard to follow. "I'm here to play a game," I said.

"What about the fact that you were hired to be an

alternate for Tuesday?"

"I don't care," I said.

"Do you actually not care?" they asked.

"I actually don't care." I walked away.

And it was true. I actually didn't care… What was done was done… now, I had to focus on myself. It was impossible to know who was telling me the truth, who was deceiving me, who was trying to use me for their own gain.

It didn't matter. I couldn't let the complicated lives of other people stop me from living out my own dreams.

I did my warmup quietly with my team. The media was there, surrounding us, even though there were seven other teams warming up in that massive room. Cameras were on Billie Rae. They were on Bruce. They were on me. It was midway through warmups when a few members of HGA showed up to watch the first rounds of the day. Franklin was there, and he was swarmed by cameras.

It was starting to feel more like we were on The Real Housewives of League of Legends, and not at a professional gaming tournament.

I tried to ignore it all. I had to focus on my first game.

And that first game was against one of the oldest teams in the country: Canuck Gaming.

It was a best-of-three, and it was off to an awkward start. During out champion selection stage, we hardly spoke. Usually, that was the time to talk strategies, but now, nobody wanted to pipe up, knowing our voices were being broadcast. It was just wretchedly uncomfortable. Bruce picked his hero without consulting the rest of us. Gobbler picked a support hero accordingly. Then, Race-Star picked a hero that did not compliment Bruce or Gobbler; it was a faux-pas that would have been avoided with a tiny bit of communication.

Billie Rae went ahead and picked her favourite mid champion, forcing me to pick a champion that complimented it, even though it wasn't my strongest jungle champion—and it did not compliment the other teammates. It was a communication disaster— but luckily, Canuck Gaming was well beyond their prime, still made up of the same members that were on the team eight years earlier. Their mid-lane player wasn't even ranked in the top 8000 anymore. Their team hadn't passed the round-robin stage of any tournament more than once in the past three years. So we were still able to win... but it was close.

We were all quiet after the game. There were so

many stupid mistakes, and we were lucky to have skirted away with a win.

But we made all the same mistakes, still not talking. I could tell that Gobbler wasn't happy about the news, about the drama. He wasn't his usual spunky self. He looked embarrassed, keeping his head down between games, when the photographers were allowed to take to the stage.

We won that next game, thanks to a bunch of dumb mistakes made by the other team—and thanks to Billie Rae playing a solid game at mid. We beat Canuck Gaming handily, but we were still quiet.

We had a two-hour break before we went to face Winnipeg E-Sports, a team making its first-ever appearance at a professional tournament. It was also our team's first appearance, but we had team members with lots of experience; they were all brand new to the scene. They made mistakes. They should have been easy to beat... but they took us out in game-one, because we simply weren't communicating.

"Come on, guys," Gobbler groaned between games. "We can't lose this one. This should be a free win."

"Says you," Race-Star said. "You were the one up at top when we were trying to push mid."

"Nobody said we were trying to push mid!" Gobbler cried.

"Is your mini-map broken or something? It was pretty obvious."

"If you don't say the plan, how am I supposed to follow it? And what was John doing in the enemy jungle at the end? We knew they had an Evelyn. That was just suicide."

"Sorry," I said. "I thought you had eyes on her."

"When did I say I had eyes on her?" he growled.

"Exactly," Billie Rae finally chimed in. "You didn't say anything. Nobody said anything. Nobody is talking. Nobody knows what to do. It's just chaos."

"I didn't hear you talking," Race-Star said.

"Let's just stop fighting," I said. "We need to win this game."

"If we're going to win, you need to get those early picks—and stop letting them get our buffs," Gobbler said.

"Then stay on top of putting down wards," I said. "That's your job."

"It's not my job when I have to keep our tank healed and buffed!"

"Then maybe Bruce should be picking a champion that needs less support!" Billie Rae said.

"Why are you taking his side?" Gobbler asked. "Hoping he buys you an Amazon Gift Card?"

Billie Rae gasped.

"Greg," Bruce said.

"What?" Gobbler said. "You're letting John accuse me of losing that game. It just seems like you're taking his side because you're afraid he's going to walk after what came out. It's just some sort of ass-kissing contest now... and you're happy to throw me under the bus to win those brownie points. But guess what? I'm not going to let you use me to manipulate him. I'm not playing along with your little game."

"Greg, calm down," Bruce growled, trying to remind him that our voices were being broadcast.

"Don't tell me to calm down," Gobbler said. "This whole thing is a fucking joke. I've never been more humiliated in my life. You know my grandmother called me this morning. Even she heard the news! This team is a literal joke."

"Greg, calm down!" Bruce roared suddenly.

But now, it was time to pick champions. The time for coming up with a strategy had passed... It was my turn to pick first, so I picked my champion. There wasn't much discussion; every time we started to talk strategies, it quickly turned into a fight about the ongoing controversy. Billie Rae wasn't talking now, after Gobbler brought up the Amazon Gift Card scandal.

And I still hadn't forgotten about her keeping my fate with the team a secret. I was still angry with her —angry enough that I saw an opportunity to get a bit of revenge…

We were winning. Bruce was playing a fierce game, being his usual self. He didn't need a team behind him to be the best. We had good momentum… but Billie Rae was making stupid mistakes. I bailed her out of one ambush that she walked right into, and now, she was walking into another one.

A part of me wanted to just let her get killed. The extra kill wouldn't have made much difference to the game outcome. Killing Billie Rae wouldn't have given them the momentum they needed to take the lead. But it would have crushed her score, which was currently mediocre at best. An additional death would have dropped her in the rankings, and then, if Centennial ended up dissolving, there would be even less of a chance of her being scouted by a team. Knowing that there was a very good chance the team would dissolve after this, it made our individual scores even more important. There were teams looking to fill spots, but they weren't going to take players who performed lousily in their last tournament appearances. They were going to go for guys like Bruce, like Race-Star—and even like Gobbler: guys who put up big numbers but lost because the weak links on their past teams were just too weak. Maybe I was even one of those worthy guys…

I didn't let them kill Billie Rae, even though I felt like she didn't deserve to be bailed out. I just wanted to secure that victory. I wanted to prove to myself that I wasn't going to stoop to the same level as her: I wasn't willing to throw someone else under the bus for my own betterment, to make myself look better.

And, I felt like she'd been through enough.

Maybe she deserved some punishment for what she did, or maybe she didn't; that wasn't for me to decide; that was for God to decide.

I killed two of the players trying to ambush her. She got away, but I wasn't so lucky. They killed me— but they all scurried off, injured, needing to retreat to heal. While they were healing, Bruce launched a hard attack, taking out two towers. They weren't strong enough to fight him back—not until their two dead players respawned.

So essentially, I sacrificed myself to win the game, though the stats on the screen didn't reflect that. Bruce took the glory and Billie Rae slipped away without the stats to show her huge blunder.

We were now 2-0 in the round-robin: one win away from guaranteeing a spot in the quarter finals. There was no free pass to the semi-finals this time. But more wins in the round-robin would get us a better seed, placing us against a weaker team in our quarter final match.

We were given another hour to break, so we went upstairs to the player lounge. All of the other players on their break looked at us, staring at us like we were a group of total losers. They began to giggle and whisper amongst one another. Our reputations were already tainted.

We tried to find a spot away from the others. We tried not to make eye-contact. We tried to remain silent, knowing there were other players eager to eavesdrop on us—and even the staff at the event.

"Did you see that the story made the front page of E-Sports Worldwide?" Race-Star said, but nobody answered him. "They have a poll up asking if we should be allowed to continue competing." We continued to ignore him. We were all sick of the drama. "The poll isn't looking good so far. The comments are worse."

"Drop it!" Bruce snapped suddenly. The whole room turned silent. Now, every player in that place was staring at us. Bruce covered the side of his face with his hand. "We're 2-0. Let's just focus on winning one more game. We need to start communicating. We've gotten lucky up until this point. We're not going to stay on a lucky streak. Let's just win this next game so we can all relax and regroup."

We pulled it together just enough to pull out one more win. The communication was still rough, but improving. It seemed like we were getting into a bit of a groove. We lost the first round but took the next two. Before exiting the stage, one of the players on the other team stood up and said, "You guys shouldn't even be allowed to play in this tournament! It's a fucking disgrace to the sport!"

"Shove it up your ass, loser!" Gobbler shouted back.

"Fuck you!"

Bruce pulled Gobbler away. "Ignore him. He's just tilted." For the other team, it meant being eliminated. It was their third consecutive loss, meaning they were now out of being able to make the quarter final round.

"Your team is a joke to the league!" the angry player shouted as his own teammates dragged him off the stage.

I have to admit that it sucked, knowing that most of the players at that tournament felt the same way. Very few of them thought that we deserved to be playing. They all thought Billie Rae should have been banned from competing for what she did when she was a teenager, playing StarCraft... what she *supposedly* did. They thought our team should have been expelled for the shady contract that screwed over Franklin—and it would have screwed me over had Tuesday stuck around.

Now, as we awaited our fourth round of round-robin, I found myself looking at Billie Rae. I watched her from across our green room. She just sat quietly, pensive, staring off into nothingness... She was probably considering her future possibilities. Maybe she was thinking about tapping out, leaving.

Bruce left the room to take a phone call. Now, Gobbler was standing up and pacing around the room. "Fuck this shit," he said. "This is a joke. I didn't grind for five fucking years to be treated like this. My reputation is practically ruined. At least if I were to walk away now, I can save a bit of face... Honestly, we should all walk together. Let's face it; it's not like we're winning this tournament. We're not beating Tri-Force Gaming, and we're not beating HGA. It would take a miracle to make it past the quarters..."

"We're not staging a walk-off," Race-Star said.

"Well, if I go, it's over anyway," Gobbler said. "A team needs six players to participate. If I leave, that leaves five. Then it's over."

"Gobbler, go for a walk," I said. "Let off some steam."

"Don't talk to me like a child," he growled at me.

"Let's just focus on getting a better seed," Race-Star said, taking over as captain during Bruce's absence. "Let's get lunch and then we'll all be in a better mood."

Food was free for players. We had access to all of

the food trucks. The food was actually amazing, and getting some food in my stomach really did make my mind clearer. I found myself remembering my whole conversation with Tuesday. I remembered her offer. I remembered that there was a new team waiting for me in Quebec: one built by gamers, and not by a millionaire with financial interests. It really did seem like a perfect chance to get away from the drama...

The drama was killing me. Well, it was killing everyone else—and their sour moods were taking me down with them. I hated all of that pessimism. I hated the vitriol. I hated that toxic environment. I knew that I couldn't stay on that team, whether Billie Rae was lying or telling the truth.

And then I remembered Tuesday's little date proposition. She wanted to see me outside of that gaming environment. She even hinted at the fact she was searching for something serious, something long-term. She knew me well enough after living with me for a few weeks... and she actually liked me enough to make that proposition.

Tuesday was really beautiful—and I was reminded of that a few minutes later when I saw her face on the cover of E-Sports Weekly, fresh off the press, being circulated around that stadium. 'A NEW

TEAM?' the headline read. And then the magazine went on to talk about all of the drama with Billie Rae and Centennial. I didn't read the articles… but I did find myself staring at Tuesday, with her long blonde hair.

She was beautiful… maybe she didn't attract me the same way Billie Rae attracted me, but I couldn't deny that she was beautiful. She was a sweet, soft-spoken girl. Maybe that was better. Maybe I didn't know much about her… but she was offering something that seemed more like stability.

I remembered something else she said: that little warning she left me with: "If Centennial signs some high-calibre player—even someone past their prime like me—just be on high alert." It was only a few minutes later when Bruce found us and said, "I have some good news. I just got off the phone with Joker's manager. He's interested in coming to play with us."

My heart fluttered cold. Joker was a former world champion. He'd competed at every major event, and won many of them. He played for Team Liquid; no team had more awards. He'd been on the cover of E-Sports Weekly many times. He had a stream that pulled in tens of thousands of viewers, even though he'd been out of the competitive scene for a few years. He was one of those past-his-prime players, coming back for a little renaissance. "He's going to play a fill-in role," Bruce continued. He eyed me for a quick moment before looking away with a guilty sort of glance.

And I knew why he was guilty...

Because Joker made his career as a jungler, like me.

Now, Tuesday's warning was loud in my mind: be on high alert if they bring in another marquee player, even if that player is beyond their prime.

Bruce was going ahead with the plan, despite the drama that Tuesday and Franklin stirred up when they left. Bruce didn't seem to really care about the controversies; he was committed to the plan, hell or high water.

"He'll be arriving tonight. I'll meet him at the airport and then we'll have a group meeting at the hotel before we split up for the night."

"Wait," Billie Rae said. "Why are we bringing him in?"

"We need the security," Bruce said. "We can't be playing with a minimum roster. If just one player on our team steps away for any reason: health, personal, family emergency... that's it: we're out." He eyed me again, as if he was insinuating I might leave. I'm guessing that he was still mad that I skipped out on the press conference.

But the other players on the team were happy about the new addition. There weren't red flags going off in their minds. They were just happy to have another star player on the team, someone who could share their experience with the rest of us, like Tuesday was doing before she made her exit.

We played our next best-of-three against a team called The Maritime Gaming Association. They beat us in two quick games, but we rebounded and won our final best-of-three against the Polar Gamers. Though we would have probably been better off losing and getting a different seed for the quarter, because we were informed before leaving the stadium that we would be facing Horizon Gaming in our quarter final: a rematch against Franklin, who was surely going to do everything he could to defeat us.

CHAPTER 17

*J*oker was a nice guy, but that warning was still chiming in my head on repeat. He was about my age, which was nice. He was calm and level-headed. He told us about a controversy that his team was wrapped up in. "People will forget all about it after a few days. It's not as big of a deal as you all think it is right now," he told us. He had a way of bringing a calmness to the team… everyone but me.

But I wasn't feeling so calm. Yes, he often played the role of tank, sometimes middle-lane, and sometimes he even played ADC—but he was primarily a jungler. His professional career was in the jungle. He was there to replace me. And I didn't want to look like a fool by sticking around, just to be swapped out when the real action started.

I went to Bruce's room before it was time to sleep. I knocked on the door and he answered. He stared at me for a long moment and said, "What is it?"

"Am I playing tomorrow?"

He paused for a moment. "Of course you are," he said.

"Tell me honestly. I don't want to look like an idiot when I'm caught off-guard."

"Why wouldn't you play?"

"You know why," I said.

He sighed and shook his head. "You're over-thinking this. We needed another player, and he was the best on the market, John. It was a business move. And I get why you might be feeling a bit scarred from the whole Tuesday business. But John—that's just business. You need to realize that this shit isn't personal. The pro gaming industry is a business at the end of the day. What? Do you think this stuff doesn't happen in hockey? Do you think it doesn't happen between MLB teams? It's a business, and you need to realize that these teams exist to make money. Sometimes that means winning games. Sometimes it means branding."

"WHAT ARE YOU SAYING?" I said, biting my tongue. I was trying to keep my cool. My focus was on winning games, not getting into the drama... but I couldn't just ignore what was happening. It seemed likely that this was all happening to replace me.

"I'm just telling you the truth, John," he said. "This is a business. Nothing more, nothing less. Now, that said—no, John. I'm not bringing Joker in to replace you. I'm bringing him in because he's the best on the market right now. I'm bringing him in because we need an alternate—because right now, it's looking like Gobbler is walking, and if he would have walked before Joker got here, it would have been the end of the line. I'm bringing Joker in because I got a call from Horatio telling me we had the budget to bring in name talent.

"And I'll tell you one other thing, John, because I like you, despite what you think: if Horatio gives me the order to swap Joker for you, I'll do it, because he's my boss—and he's technically your boss to. As for who I'm going to make the main—whoever is better. Now, between you and me—because I like you—Joker isn't going to be taking your spot unless it's a direct order from Horatio, because Joker isn't what he used to be. He's not a top player. He's more of a streamer. And if I'm going to be swapping him in, it will be into a support role, because Gobbler just hasn't been pulling his weight."

Now, Bruce was staring bluntly at me. I was trying to get a read on him. I was trying to understand how I fit into this puzzle.

His eyes narrowed. "John, did you, by chance, speak with Tuesday before she left town?"

"Maybe," I said. "I'm free to talk to whoever I want to talk to."

"Yes," he said. "But she's technically not. She signed an NDA. Franklin did the same, and now,

Horatio is proceeding with legal action. The details in those contracts weren't to be discussed outside of the walls of the team house. And it's come to my attention that Tuesday is launching a new team. She's approached a few of our team members, trying to poach them. She's also approached our sponsors, which is a serious violation of the contract she's legally bound to."

This was new information to me, and I wasn't sure how to process it... and it was only about to get even more complicated.

"Want to know how I know that she's poached other team members?" Bruce continued.

"How?" I asked softly.

"Race-Star came to me two days ago and showed me the text messages between them. Tuesday was offering sexual favours if Race would travel out to Quebec to be on her new team. I saw the texts with my own eyes, John. And that's just a warning to you, as a friend, because I don't know what she said to you. I like you. But I'll say it again: the pro gaming industry is a business, and it's filled with hustlers. Money makes the decisions here, not people."

Gobbler didn't show up at the stadium the next morning. Bruce told us that he got onto a plane early that morning to return to Alberta, to collect his things from the team house. He was leaving the team —not interested in facing Franklin on that stage. "He's under the impression that he's protecting his reputation," Bruce said to us. "Joker will be filling in as support."

Joker perked right up. He was a tall guy, with round glasses, scruffy hair, and a crooked smile. "I won't let you down."

Then, Bruce turned to Billie Rae. "I'm making a hard decision today," he said. "Billie Rae, you're going to be sitting the first game out. I'm putting Kitten in on mid."

Billie Rae turned white, but said nothing. The news was a complete shock.

"Kitten has been putting up amazing numbers in practise. I think she deserves the shot."

"Kitten doesn't play mid," I said.

"She has before," Bruce said without looking at me. "And she will today. I'll be honest with you all: Franklin knows Billie Rae's tactics too well. If we're going to beat HGA this time, we need to change things up."

"Bruce…" I said.

He turned to look at me. "What is it?"

I wanted to remind him about Billie Rae's contract. Was he allowed to pull her out? Was I allowed to comment on the contract that I was technically not supposed to know about? Well—everyone knew about it now, including the fans in the stands.

"Well?" he said.

I looked at Billie Rae. I saw the devastation on her face. She was unable to speak up for herself, so I felt like I needed to… but what could I say? "I think Billie Rae would be fine on mid. She's our best mid."

She looked at me, now turning a shade of pink.

"It might get some of the media pressure off if we bench her," Race-Star suggested.

"But she's the best mid at this tournament. We'd be making a huge mistake by benching her," I insisted. "And I play better with her. I've never played better in my life than I have with her on mid."

Billie Rae was now staring into my eyes, seemingly shocked that I would defend her.

"I want Billie on mid," I said. "I have nothing against Kitten, but I don't have the same connection with Kitten."

"Kitten will play mid," Bruce said firmly.

"That's ridiculous," I said.

"John!" Bruce snapped.

Now, everyone was glaring at me.

I shook my head. "This all just seems like a PR

move. I don't think the quarter final is the time to be worrying about optics."

"You're here to do a job, John. When you're captain, you can make the decisions. Right now, I'm making this decision, whether it's right or wrong."

So we played without Billie Rae. I sat next to a very nervous Kitten Krusader, who had absolutely no tournament experience at all, and now she was being tasked with winning a best-of-five so we could avoid elimination, so we could all keep our jobs, because we all knew that Horatio would dissolve the team if we didn't advance to the World Circuit.

We won the first game thanks to a faux-pas by Griswold Gamer. He tried to sneak through our jungle to join an ambush, and I caught him with a snare. Because of his failure to join that ambush, the whole ambush failed, with Race-Star killing three of their teammates. Suddenly, we had all of the experience and money that we needed to steamroll through the rest of that match.

We won our second game, with Bruce playing like a juggernaut, brute forcing his way down his lane, gaining disgusting experience and money with flawless play after flawless play.

We only needed one more win to make it through to the semi-final… but that win never came.

Franklin stepped up his game and destroyed Kitten at mid in that third game: killing her three consecutive times, which was enough to make him overpowered for the rest of the game. Then, his team rallied in the fourth game to tie the series: an all-around impressive play.

It came down to that final game: an intense hour-long back-and-forth. We didn't lose because of Kitten Krusader. It wasn't my fault that we lost, or even Joker, who hardly knew our play-style. Amazingly, we lost that game because Bruce made a series of dumb mistakes. It happens to everyone from time to time, even the best of the best like Bruce…

We were eliminated. We weren't going through to the World Circuit.

We were silent. The energy was simply gone. We stuck around for a few hours, doing the press conference, answering some fan questions… and then we went back to the hotel. We were stuck in Vancouver until Monday, but nobody wanted to go back to the stadium. Bruce locked himself up in his room and wouldn't come out, but Race-Star told us that he'd been crying; they shared a room.

"I guess the team is over," Race-Star said as we met for breakfast the next morning. "I mean, unless Horatio has some change of heart, I guess." He was referring to the fact that Horatio had a number of failed teams in his past.

"We'll all land on new teams," Kitten said. "We made it pretty deep." It was the first sign of optimism—and she even had a small smile on her face. It was nice to hear a bit of positivity; we really had made it further than anyone expected. We were one win away from making the semi finals. We were two days of winning away from making the World Circuit as Canada's top team.

But now, we would be going home to uncertainty. We would all be on the hunt for new teams… or maybe just new jobs in general. There was a Game Stop in Red Deer, not too far from where we'd been living. I think I saw a NOW HIRING sign in the window… maybe that was part of my future.

Billie Rae wouldn't have to worry too much; all of the drama from the weekend had a strangely positive impact on her streaming account. Her followers surged by over one-hundred thousand. Maybe it's true: no press is bad press. She wasn't even getting hate-mail concerning the allegations… well, not much of it, anyway. The main takeaway that the public got from all of the headlines was, 'hey, there's a hot E-girl who streams in lingerie!'. Nobody cared about the drama outside of those of us inside that industry.

In fact, she did her first post-incident stream on Monday night, after we got back to Alberta. 125,000 people tuned in, and she earned over $600—and it wasn't even a lingerie stream. That kind of cash in a town like Red Deer will go a long way…

Race-Star would be fine; he posted great numbers at both the Qualifier and at Nationals. His stats had him in the top 750. Bruce was in the top 300.

Kitten had even cracked the top 1000. And, as a girl, she didn't have anything to worry about. Many teams had gender diversity quotas, and would jump at any female on the market in the top 2000—never mind the top 1000.

My future seemed a bit less certain. Sure, I'd cracked into the top 1000, meaning I could go to the individual tournaments (if I could find a sponsor to pay for my travel expenses). There was a good chance that I would attract the attention of pro teams by playing those highly-ranked matches… but I still didn't have the name that the others had.

That Monday night, while Bruce was outside having a cigarette, Race-Star addressed the elephant in the room: "Has anyone had offers from other teams yet?"

We were all silent... at first. Then, Kitten piped up. "Liquid messaged me about their B-team last night. They want to give me a tryout."

"Shit! Liquid!?" Joker said, eyes beaming. "You gotta do it, girl."

"Well, it's their B-team," Kitten blushed.

"Whatever. I've been to the B-team house. They have a pool—and a theatre room! They throw the craziest parties. It's like living at the Playboy mansion."

Kitten smiled and shrugged her shoulders. "I'm considering it. Please don't tell Bruce."

"Of course not," Race-Star said. "I got an offer from HGA." I suppose I should now point out that HGA won Nationals and qualified for the World Circuit. "They want me to be their ADC alt, but they said I would definitely get playtime in round-robin —and maybe more if I performed well."

"Good for you!" Kitten gasped.

Joked gave him a pat on the back. "They're a real powerhouse this year, bro," he laughed. "Good for you."

Then, eyes turned to me. "What about you, Johnny?" asked Race-Star. "Any inquiries?"

I thought about telling them about Tuesday's new team… but I remembered what Bruce told me, about Tuesday offering Race-Star sexual favours. I didn't want to go from one sham team to another… Plus, I didn't speak French, so living in Quebec City wasn't exactly a dream. "Nothing," I said.

"Something will come," Race-Star said, and then Bruce came back in, so the conversation ended.

Billie-Rae streamed that night while we practised, though we weren't too sure why we were practising anymore. It didn't seem like we were working on team tactics; we were all just playing together, doing whatever we wanted—worrying more about our own ranks than our performance as a team.

The next morning, I woke up to a message from Canuck Gaming—not the best team, but they were interested in 'chatting'. They wanted to set a date to talk. I was excited by the opportunity, even though I didn't see them as a legitimate competitor. But I knew that members of their team got paid; they made their living playing; their sponsors sent them to tournaments: team, and individual. So maybe it was a good place to start. Maybe I didn't need to set my sights on the world's best team just yet.

Well, it was all irrelevant, because that afternoon, there was a knock at the door. The person didn't wait for Bruce to answer before coming in, because the person owned the house: it was Horatio.

He had a smile on his face, and two men standing behind him holding large gift baskets. They all came in and placed the baskets down on the tables. The two helpers went to fetch more bags from the black Suburban parked on the street. "I'm just in town to congratulate my favourite group of gamers," he said.

We were all silent. We all surely had the same thought in our heads: was he here to pull the plug? Was he there to tell Bruce that it was all over?

He shook our hands and congratulated us for a thrilling season. "I wish we could have gone to the World Circuit," he said. "But we'll make that our goal for next year. I'm just thrilled that we made it as far as we did. And the sponsors are thrilled too."

"T—They are?" Bruce said. He was apparently more stunned than the rest of us.

Horatio smiled and nodded his head. "They upped their investments. You guys really put on an impressive show." He looked at me and smiled. "I was watching some of your picks in jungle, J-Rock. That was just... awesome!"

"Thanks," I said softly.

"Well, I got the e-mail this morning from the Canadian E-Sports Federation. We have our qualifier invite stamped for next year, so I guess we need to start training. Bruce, I want to talk to you upstairs about finding a final alt to fill out the team."

"O—Okay," Bruce said.

"The rest of you, I came with gifts. And one other thing! There's a contractor coming by this afternoon to look at the back yard. We're putting in a pool, and a bar. And I think I want to redo the exterior of the house in black. What do you think? Black is cool, right?"

We were all just silent, stunned. It wasn't at all what any of us expected. We watched Horatio take Bruce upstairs. We remained silent for a minute, and then we all approached those gift bags.

Again, they were filled with extravagant gifts: chocolates, liquor, gift cards... and then there was the expensive stuff: watches for the boys, jewellery for the girls. "Oh my God," Billie Rae gasped, holding up a shining gold card, that looked a bit too wide to be a credit card.

"What is that?" I asked.

"It's a certificate for... a boob job," she said. She blushed and smiled. "It's worth eighteen-thousand dollars."

I had no idea if that was appropriate or not... but Billie Rae had talked about wanting to have larger breasts. She had her small perky tits from taking HRT for years. Maybe Horatio was paying for her breast enlargement because he knew it would bring in more viewers onto her stream, thus more fans for the team... or maybe he was just supporting her transition. I suppose it was something we would never know for sure, but nobody was upset about it —especially not me, because that evening, Billie Rae told me that I would get to play with them when she got them done.

In my basket, I found a stack of plane tickets and some paperwork. Horatio had booked me flights to all of the major individual championships. My teammates had tickets too, for many of the same competitions: hotels booked, credit cards to use for meals and expenses.

I nearly cried with joy, but I held back the tears, wanting to look somewhat masculine. Billie Rae ran to me and threw her arms around me, squeezing me. The others rejoiced, still stunned. We did have that obvious discussion, wondering if this meant that the team would really continue to exist, or if this was just a temporary stint to improve optics after the scandals that came out the previous week.

But really, those scandals were all blown out of proportion, and exaggerated grossly. I'd spent lots and lots of time thinking about it all. Was I upset that Billie Rae didn't tell me that I was doomed to be an alt? Of course I wished she would have told me, but she would have been facing a lawsuit if I left the team in a fit, like Franklin did. Now, Franklin was facing a half-million dollar lawsuit, and it wasn't looking like he was going to win. Tuesday was facing a similar lawsuit, and with the text messages that Race-Star had on his phone, it just wasn't looking good.

Billie Rae was just keeping promises that she'd made (she told me about Franklin, and that was probably the closest she could could safely come to telling me that I was in a similar position).

Bruce was just keeping his promises too, being loyal to the man who gave him a team and was funding his lifelong dream of being a captain. And could Horatio really be blamed for the secret contracts? Like Bruce said: it was just business.

I suppose one could argue in favour or against what Horatio did. It became a regular debate in the house, whenever Bruce was away for whatever reason.

It was hard to be mad when the man was funding my career, putting me up in a house, and giving me opportunities that I'd only ever dreamed of before.

And, because of him, I got to live with Billie Rae, who was also happier than she'd ever been in her life.

The odd article would come out from time to time… and interviewers would want to come to our house to talk about all of those old controversies. They were seemingly baffled that everyone stuck around, except for Gobbler. But they didn't know the reality of the situation. They didn't understand that one important thing: it was all business. And that was something we were all learning in that house.

I went to Japan for my first Individual Cup Qualifier. I came third out of one-hundred competitors. I scored big points. When I returned home, Billie Rae was waiting for me, in her room, in lingerie, with her new breasts. "They're sore, so be gentle," she whispered with a grin.

Being gentle wasn't so easy, but I did my best—and she did her best when she was being me, gripping me by the hips, pushing deep into my body. It was fun, but it was much more fun two weeks later, when she was allowed to really go at it.

I was one of the top seeds at the first major World tournaments, and I placed second-place, winning my first $100,000. As per my contract, which was standard, 20% of that went to the team fund. But still: $80,000 went into my bank account, and that put a big smile on my face. I took Billie Rae out on some nice dates.

It was a blissful year. It often felt like a dream. But it really turned into a dream the next year, when we went to our first National Qualifiers and won, getting a spot at Nationals, straight past the round-robin stage. Then, we won Nationals, beating Horizon 3-0 in a best-of-five. We had our pass to the World Circuit.

And to complete the fairy tale, we won the Moscow tournament: a $5,000,000 prize, and a trophy that was so heavy, it took three of us to hoist it up for photos. I can assure you that I had a name after that—and Billie Rae had the respect that she'd deserved all along.

THE END

FIND ME ON PATREON!

I really hope that you're enjoying my work! I've been fortunate enough to make this my full-time job for the past couple of years, though it hasn't been easy. There's a lot of financial uncertainty as a full-time self-published writer.

I would feel tremendously blessed if you would venture on over to my Patreon page and consider supporting me there. I think you will be excited by what I have to offer: **a community, free book chapters, pictures, contests, commissions, free stories, advanced releases, and much more**. It's the only way to get your hands on these exclusive titles:

THE PUNISHMENT
FORCED

TWINS
LORI'S LAST FUCK
THE GIRL TWIN (A Full-Length Novel)
TRANS CAM WHORE
GETTING READY FOR PROM
DUBIOUS CONSENT
PETRA'S FRISKY PHOTOSHOOT
JILLIAN'S 14 INCHES

And for as little as a dollar per month—is that even a quarter cup of Starbucks coffee?
Be the gorgeous, filthy doll you know that you are and come hang out with me:

https://www.patreon.com/nikkicrescent

NEWSLETTER

JOIN NIKKI CRESCENT'S MAILING LIST!

Thank you for picking up one of my books! Chances are I'm in the process of working on another one! Hey—Did you know that you can read my whole catalogue free if you subscribe to **Kindle Unlimited**? It's true! If you aren't subscribed, I would highly recommend it.

I have started this little newsletter to let all of my beautiful readers know when I'm offering discounts, releasing new books, and giving away **EXCLUSIVE CONTENT FOR FREE**. The sign up takes about four seconds (seriously). I will never share your email address with anyone, you will never receive any spam, and you can unsubscribe at any time with the click of a single button.

CLICK HERE TO SIGN UP FOR NIKKI CRESCENT'S MAILING LIST NOW!

Can't open the link? Copy and paste this link into your browser:

http://eepurl.com/O3CKz

ABOUT THE AUTHOR

NIKKI CRESCENT

Nikki Crescent is a young writer from the golden prairies of Alberta, Canada. She spent her schooling years lost in her own imagination, writing everything from articles, screenplays, comic books, and short stories. Obsessed with the idea of love, fascinated with sex and captivated with the art of writing, Nikki decided to become a writer of erotic romance.

Nikki Crescent is a top-selling writer of romantic and erotic fiction with over two hundred and fifty titles across many sub-genres. Her fiction work has found her on Amazon's best-selling charts many times over.

Made in the USA
Las Vegas, NV
01 August 2024

93223910R40152